ORION'S BELT

DENBY MONTANA

Celtic Butterfly Press

First published in Oakland, CA, 1994 by Spellman-Tris
This edition published 2015 by Celtic Butterfly
Celtic Butterfly is an imprint of Spellman-Tris. For information
address: Spellman-Tris, PO Box 1303, Alameda, CA 94501

The characters and events in this book are fictitious. Any similarity to real persons, living or dead, is coincidental and not intended by the author.

The cover photograph was taken over a country road in the Republic of Ireland.

This edition includes the omitted story "Orion's Belt".

Denby Montana is a pseudonym for Owen Mould

ISBN 10:9644856-9-9
ISBN 13: 978-0-9644856-9-3

Printed in Book Antiqua typeface

Forever thanks to the Angels at
The Berkeley Housing Authority
Highland Hospital Emergency
and
Fred Finch Youth Center

Table of Contents

2 KILLERS...1

THE ALBATROSS...11

THE BROKER 25

DANA & ALLEN...37

SWITCH...49

THE LAST ELIGIBLE BACHELOR IN SAN

FRANCISCO...63

THE ANGEL...73

THE DISCORDANT PIANO.....................87

THE PAPERCLIP MAN.....................97

THE MASTER BAKERS....................105

THE COLLEAGUES....................117

BIG RED.............................131

INCUBUS...........................145

ORION'S BELT.....................155

THE STARS OF ORION

The constellation of Orion consists primarily of the following 7 stars: Betelgeuse, Bellatrix, Rigel and Saiph. The "belt" consists of the three stars, Alnitak, Alnilam, and Mintaka.

Subsidiary stars not always visible "flesh out" the figure. Meissa forms the head. The bright Orion Nebula, M42, marks the point of the object that appears to hang from belt level. The stars that comprise his left arm and shield are called Tabit and Pi1 through Pi6. His upraised right arm consists of stars that can be considered part of Gemini.

ORION'S BELT

2 KILLERS

The last contestant left in a hail of back slaps and towel snaps to the rear. All the spectators, girlfriends and home-boys had left long ago and the gymnasium lights dimmed down as a few waste papers skittered across the floor to the gust of a door slammed by a ref loaded with karate flags and papers, but Chip still sat in the locker room, head in his hands.

*When all was quiet, he got up and made a phone call to Suzette, telling her that he would be in late. Out drinking with the boys. She told him not to drink too much; she'd be up reading a book or something and the balm would be waiting there on the table. It was the Deet Jah Yao. He said that was fine. She asked if he needed tape or iodine or gauze this time . . . and he said, no. No cuts; just only forms tonight. Just the balm would be fine. Okay, good, she said. She wanted to finish the chapter and get started on a new one. Fine, he said. She would be up late anyway. Okay, he said. I'll put out the balm she said. Thanks, he said. The operator disconnected them and the dial tone filled the line. He hung up and leaned against the wall.

He felt tired. He would have to take the bus tonight since messing up the car. Better he didn't drive anyway; lately he had been dropping things like the vase. Last week he had skipped out on all his classes in the City. The balm was a good thing: to be there, waiting for him. A lot of things broke easily or didn't work, but there were good things that did work, that still worked and the balm was one of them. It was always there, reliable in how it worked in the deep tissues, always a surprise somehow. Fuck, he loved that fucking balm.

Chip was a fighter and he felt off balance.

He pulled away from the wall and stood the way he should on both feet, but he still did not feel right. Maybe because he hadn't sparred tonight. He was not fighting anyone tonight, not anyone. Because of the fear and he knew it was because of the fear. Not the fear of losing or the punishment hit, not those things. It was the fear of losing the focus when every single move had to be precisely correct. Because he was afraid, he lost focus, his moves could not be precise, and because he lost focus, he felt off balance. No one had said anything to him. No one had looked at him, knowing the truth with fear or stupid awe, which he hated more than the fear. He hated that artificial respect that was not respect for the man and his actions, but the sheep-like awe of stupid ignorance. Stupid, stupid, stupid.

He heard a rustling and turned, knees flexed, up on the balls of his feet, but it was only an old man with a broom, knocking a ball of wrapping tape from under the bench.

Chip did not say anything. The old man kept sweeping the little ball until it rolled in front of the trash bin. Then he gave it a sharp tap and the ball leapt up with sudden energy into the bin.

"Not bad," commented Chip.

"I'm getting too old to pick up things," the man said.

"What are you doing this stuff for then?"

"I will tell you," said the man. "Why are you here?"

"Whirlpool," Chip said. "I'm going now." Chip moved toward his bag and grabbed the handle.

"I heard you on the telephone."

"Yeah. Gotta move on it." Chip moved toward the exit.

"People are not supposed to die in this sport, are they? That's not the point." The man's intonation suggested more of a statement than a question.

Chip stopped and turned and said, "That's right." Then he said, "What are they saying about it?"

"I don't give a damn what anybody is saying," said the man. "Neither should you. That's not the point either. Who is your opponent?"

"Anybody who faces me," said Chip and he turned to go, opening the door.

"No wonder you feel stupid. You talk like a damn fool." The old man followed him out and added, quietly, "Nakayama is upset."

This made Chip turn and drop his bag in the hall to face the man, whose lower body was diagonally slashed by the one light still burning in the hall. Chip asked the man who he was and the man responded, "That's my business. I am simply here. Come with me. Come on!"

Chip and the old man left the gym and walked across the street to an all night Denny's, past the newspaper kiosks announcing the large mandate of the new President behind wire grills. In the brights of the diner, Chip could see the huge knuckles and hard pads of the man's hands. After the waitress set the coffee in front of them and the offer of pie was refused, the old man spoke. "You have someone waiting for you. Now you can tell the truth: you are now out drinking with one of the boys."

The man pulled a candle out of his coat pocket and set it on the counter between them. After a few sputtering snaps with a lighter, Chip got a pack of matches from the waitress and lit the candle. The man waved with his hand in a gesture that Chip was to go ahead and snuff it with one punch, but Chip said at that point, "Do we really have to do this bullshit? We're in a diner."

The man shrugged. "Nakayama's idea. Something about testing the spirit or something. I'm not into that crap myself. You a student?"

"I take classes."

"The boy takes classes; now that's precise. In what do you take classes?"

"Film."

"Film. I like strong pictures. Whaddya think about Woody Allen?"

"You mean his life or his movies," Chip added sarcastically.

"I thought that picture about the doctor was to the point. Okay, look at that woman," the man said, indicating the waitress. "What do you see?"

Chip looked at her and saw a thirty-ish Black woman, hair jeri-ed under a white cap, with a lined face that said here is a single mother with a night job and day school and two kids living in or near Section Eight. She had tear-shaped eyeglasses with rhinestone clipons hanging about her neck and a name plate that said, "Irene."

"I see a waitress," Chip said.

The man looked disappointed. "A wannabe film-maker who is loose with the truth and blind. No wonder he depends upon what people say. Deaf, blind and dumb as an ass. When I see that woman, I see my sister, who is beautiful."

"Cut the bullshit."

"I am not here to make you feel better like some new age goo-roo. You say you want to make pictures. Oh, excuse me: 'films'. Film is like anything else. Like karate or wrestling or making a clay pot or a poem. When you compete, when you film and put it out, if you pay attention to what people say, you have lost no matter how many gold-plated doorstops they give you. You make something that projects somebody else you lack the imagination to present yourself."

"This is horseshit. You are talking about stuff you don't know anything about. Allen was a genius until he got fucked up . . .".

"That's better . . . ".

"Oh fuck you. You don't know what its about."

The man's eyes flared with anger. "Listen boy. My brothers are dying on the street down in L.A. this minute. I don't have to be up here talking to some white boy feeling sorry for himself because he accidentally offed somebody. I could be down there helping my brothers and sisters survive!"

"Why did they send you?"

"I killed men. Dozens of men. I was in Korea and I saw my brothers die at Choisin Reservoir. And I have killed men . . . since then."

Irene came up to the counter. "Everything okay gentlemen?" She was looking at the man.

"We're fine!" both of them snapped at her.

"Okayyyyy . . .", she said and walked away.

"So that's why you came. For the honor and glory of the dojo . . .", Chip said.

"Now you cut the bullshit. You think you are living in some fucking movie? What kind is that? Comedy, tragedy or . . .".

"You're about as wise an old man as a tree stump."

"You are living in a movie. You expect some wiseguy to pull a sleight of hand, snatch some pebbles and give you the gift of grace packaged with a zen aphorism. Instead you got a street nigger telling you, white boy, you got to live with it and keep it from going to your fool head your entire life. Your in-tire life! It's been fifteen damn years since some West Point asshole sent us expendables to Choisin and I know it never ends. You don't make yourself feel good about it. You don't make yourself feel down about it. You don't regret it and you don't shrug it off. You live with it and you do something else other than turning to face the wall, singing a little gospel song to yourself. There is no fucking atonement! Right now you are full of yourself and your righteous self-pity fills the whole world in your head and poisons the atmosphere around it."

They had finished their coffee. Chip rolled the warm mug in his thick fingered hands, debating something in himself.

"Fuck this candle shit. Let's go."

They each lay a dollar-fifty on the counter and walked out together. "What next?" Chip said.

"What you do at the end of every workout. Come on."

"Pushups?"

The old man swore an astonishing string of obscenities that included sexual particulars of the Holy Trinity, Moses, Mohammed and denizens of Noah's ark. "No! After that!" Then he added, "Please god! Give him the gift of understanding before he makes another movie!"

They arrived at the doors to the gym. While the man jangled the keys, Chip said, "You know, the . . . boy I killed was . . .".

"I know," he said, his back turned. "That doesn't matter any more. He took his chances and it was an accident."

They went in and the man flicked up the switches. While the old fashioned gymnasium lights began to hum, crackle, and flicker before finally snapping on one after another, Chip said, "There's something else."

The old man handed him a damp towel. "What is it?"

"My father died in Korea."

The man looked at him a long time. "There's been enough dying. Let's mop up."

The two of them bent side to side and, crouching, began shoving the towels across the floor from one side to the other. At one point near the middle, the old man paused to unstick some tape from the floor boards.

"You never told me why you are doing this," Chip asked him.

The man threw the piece over to the far side. "Nakayama hates waste."

THE ALBATROSS

Long long time ago, during the Golden Age of wonders, in the days before television and memorandums, a flock of birds lived on a tropical atoll in the Sea of Tranquility near the Land of Good Herbs. Each spring the young birds would leave their nests so as to try out their new wings and receive flight instruction from an old Pelican named Griesa.

One young bird, named Edward, had been hatched late and so consequently no matter how hard he tried he was always behind everyone else. He was last to lose his down, he was last in preening class and his grades in flight theory were laughable.

"Now the reasons we fly," Griese began, "Is to eat." Old Griese stumped back and forth in lecture and shifted the shell of a razorclam from one side of his beak to the other. "The reason we stay aloft is due entirely to mechanical forces, persistent flapping, and the grace of the Great Almighty Batking. There is nothing we can do about it except flap."

"But if this is true," inquired Edward, "why do we have to go to school?"

"Edward!" Spluttered Griese. "What time did you get out of bed this morning?"

And at this, all of the young birds began chirping and twittering together, well, like a flock of birds, "Edward the bed-bird! Edward the bed-bird!" until poor Edward had to slink away.

He had watched Old Griese fly with nothing but a flurry of flaps on take-off and a dignified, regular beat while aloft. Something seemed at odds with the teacher's practice and his instructions to flap, flap, flap like mad once in the air.

From high on beaky rock, Edward watched the advanced students practice their lessons. Sparrow began wapping his wings faster and faster, going wap, wap, waprapwaprapraprapraprap until Griese shouted "Jump up ya blasted pea-brain!" Upon which sparrow leapt up and went dodging right and left a foot above the ground until he plumped bang into a hillock of tufted sand. After a beat of silence, sparrow's head popped out and shook loose a spray of dirt. One black eye blinked beneath a torn leaf of razor grass. "Good! Keep doing the same until you get it right!" shouted Griese before waddling off to his next pupil, little kiwi.

While watching his colleagues churning the sand with frenzied flaps, it occurred to Edward that there had to be a better way.

So he set off to teach himself how to fly with a minimum of effort. This necessarily involved a fair amount of trial and error, in which Edward would become airborne on brief glides before wonking into a pile of guano. One day, while watching the slow beat of Griese's flight, a leaf fell from a bush giving Edward the idea that if he wanted to soar, he needed to begin from an higher position. Hence, he found the path leading to the cliff tops. On a two day journey, with a bit of glide and hop, he made it to the point where rough jags hung out high over the beach below. There, the distant squabble of the flock reached him only as murmur. He hesitated before leaping off from so high a place, but having come so far on this journey, he realized that for him there would be no turning back. What would happen lay in the hands of a fabulous unknown destiny.

He leaped out and spread his wings. Immediately, his speed accelerated beyond what had ever been possible as gravity yanked him toward the hard sea. But then an updraft took him, the sweet wind enfolded him with supporting arms and he sailed way out in a great arc high over the ocean descending in a languorous spiral to the sea just offshore where he plopped in unceremoniously among a group of clacking mallards.

Nobody was impressed.

Although he had succeeded somewhat, the problem of climbing to the top of the cliff for each flight remained a sticky problem. Then there was the matter of the continuous free-fall, which, although gentle enough, did not entirely fit Edward's desire to remain aloft at will as long as he wanted.

Little kiwi ran by chased by the starling family who were trying to harry the little one until there was no recourse but to fly. They tormented kiwi by dropping loads of bat guano on him and kiwi looked very much a dirty bird. He was all speckled. "If you figure it out, send me a telegram! First chance I get I'm outta here!" And with that, kiwi ran off.

With each flight, Edward learned a little more. He learned to tilt his wings just so, catching the air to lift him higher. By shifting his body, turning a tail feather just a hair, he could swing wide or narrow in the opposite direction, catching updrafts he learned to read by looking at the surface of the sea, the clouds and the sun. Soon, he no longer needed to arduously climb to the cliff tops each time, as he developed his ability to ride the wind in a way that allowed the air to do all the work. His launch pads became lower and lower until with a minimum of flap he could rise from the surface of the sea swell itself.

In triumph he returned to the island to demonstrate an especially complicated triple barrel-roll. He landed in front of the great dodo who blinked at him from over the edge of his hammock slung between two trees. "You're a damn fool Edward," said the dodo. "Why bother flying when everything you need is right here." He puffed a lazy ring of smoke from his cigar. He pulled a thick gold watch from his waistcoat. "Time for a nap." he said, and he went to sleep.

Edward despaired. Almost everyone had left the island to migrate, each according to their styles as taught by Griese who shook his head. "What a hardcase you are, Edward. You'll never amount to anything. I have no idea how you are even going to feed yourself. Me, I'm going to Hawaii for the winter.

You'll never get there without flapping. And he took off.

Angrily Edward leapt up and soared way high out over the wine-dark sea. Below he saw a curious sight. It was the strangest creature he had ever seen, with what appeared to be three white wings pointing straight up out of a long body with a pointed beak, gliding along the ocean surface. When he spiraled down, he saw there were dark things with two legs running all over its back.

When he got closer he could see one of the bipeds lift up a big stick and point it at him. It was an ancient mariner of course. There was a puff of smoke and a loud bang. Suddenly Edward felt himself falling. He hit the sea and plunged beneath its surface.

A long time he rolled in green violence of sub-surface currents. "Oh gods have mercy! he said, or burbled rather. And the gods as usual, did not hear him.   They were busy arguing among themselves about where to put the next constellation in the al-ready crowded milky way. The dugong, a minion of Atlantis found Edward.

Edward was terrified. The dugong has a tail like a whale, the body of a walrus, the flippers of a penguin, the eyes of tea saucers, and the face of an old fat man who has eaten far too many cherries.

"You appear in need of assistance." mentioned the dugong. "Are you by chance edible?" When Ed-ward shook his head frantically, the dugong sighed. "Well, come along then." And he put Edward into his pocket, which was filled with air.

He brought Edward down to the palace of At-lantis, which was built entirely of living coral and which had many chambers filled with air inhabited by members of the court of Neptune. The dugong straightened his tie and brought Edward past the mother-of-pearl gates, past the octopus ticket taker and the guards with their big shark teeth, past the nautilus machines in the imperial exercise room, past the groupers gathered about the seaweed vending machines and right past His Most Celebrated Excellent Imperial Secretary Fish right into the boardroom where the King sat at the head of a long table surrounded by his Imperial Walrus Cabinet.

Atlantis was at that moment on the telephone with Jupiter. "The bottom line is that we got too many stars already. There's gonna be an industry shakeout."

"Hey who loves ya baby," said the dugong.

"Hmrumph! What? Go away; I got the Thunderer on line." said Atlantis.

"Put him on hold. I got someone in trouble and a plan that'll answer your sweetest dreams." The dugong took Edward from his pocket.

The king of the Seven Seas, Inc., glared with a single red-rimmed eye while cradling the mother of pearl hand-set.

"Listen. I got a plan that'll knock your socks off. Remember Motta?"

The Emperor of the Seas undulated along his entire length. His beard curled and uncurled all by itself and his trident rose up. "Hey, I got rush off to a meeting. I'll get a proposal to you by Freya's day and we talk again. Right." He rang off. "It's tough being a king. What is it?"

"This boy here has run into some heavy weather. I say we hire him as a messenger instead of that Mercury. Dig? You get a liaison to the South. It all goes down without any talk, cause you got your own connection, and you get points for charitable contribution. When its all over, you got your merger and still come up smelling like roses. Whaddya say, boss?"

Atlantis mulled a bit. Atlantis was, unlike Jupiter, a kind god with a soft touch for animals, and besides, Atlantis was passionately in love with Motta, goddess of the South Wind. Motta dwelt far, far to the South in the ice mansions of Antarctica, guarded by her jealous father, and she passed too quickly above the waves for Atlantis to call to her. Besides, Atlantis was bashful.

Atlantis took Edward and breathed an immortal soul into him. He clothed the bird all in white and fed him the choicest sardines from the treasury. Meanwhile he sent the dugong off to deal with the lunatic mariner who had shot Edward. There in the bubble chamber surrounded by nautilus, huge open clams and undulating sea fronds he gave Edward his charge: to go tell Motta of this love for her and that if she refused to recognize the extent of his feelings by dropping a single ice crystal into the waves, he would go down to the Kingdom of the Dark Lord and play hell's croupier with Pluto in a dice game for men's souls for eternity.

At the description of the terrible Kingdom of Dis, Edward started shaking in his feathers. Actually, Atlantis really liked Motta a lot, and was to honest to take by power what others often stole. In fact, Atlantis was really a good, old fashioned family man, and even though he was constantly surrounded by the lithe naiads, dryads and want-ads of his court he was lonely. After a thousand centuries he had been through them all three or four times already. It's tough being a king.

Edward shot up out of the water, a blazing emissary of light and began the long journey along the coast to the south, passing over the birds in their summer homes twittering and chirping mindlessly away. On the point where the last land juts out before the wide open water, he stopped to rest inside an abandoned barn. There, as he fell asleep he wondered how he was ever to find his way across the open space free of all landmarks to the Palace of Antarctica without getting lost.

In the morning, there was a rustling way up in the rafters, a nervous fluttering of wings. Eric soared up and found a white creature newly emerged from a cocoon. He had never seen one of these before and he watched as she beat her wings slowly, then suddenly took off, dodging among shafts of light standing like pillars from the floor to the torn old roof of the hall. Edward flew up through one of the vents and the creature followed. Or seemed to. It never flew a direct path, and always seemed to arrive somewhere purely by chance, without intention. She did not speak, but for the next few days she stayed by Edward, flitting here and there, but always staying close.

There began a strange communication between them, in which no sounds passed between them, which consisted of pure awareness. The creature, was pure white and fragile; she was nothing more than a scattering of dust and wings fluttering about the sailing albatross towards the south over wide, sun flecked seas. Now and then she would land on Edward's back and although he could not feel the weight, he could sense a mind whispering inside his head, "I am here."

Somehow she had a sense of what direction to go. Through her, without words, he learned the ways of the stars and how to guide himself by them at night, all without words.

Along the way, the two of them spied a derelict human ship, and coasting down to look, Edward noticed a raving old mariner chanting execrable poetry on the deck. "Water, water everywhere and not a drop to drink," the old mariner was saying. Edward circled the derelict and shrugged. Oh well, condemned to abominable verse; could have been worse. He flew off, leaving the old mariner to continue his own story.

A little further on he spied a little raft far below and swooped down for a closer look. It was the kiwi, strumming a guitar on a raft with a sail made of dodo feathers pushing him merrily along.

The song the kiwi sang went something like this:

> "Going where the weather suits my clothes.
> I'm going where the weather suits my clothes.
> Going where the weather suits my clothes,
> Hey,   hey, hey!
> I ain't gonna be treated this a-wayyyyy..."

Edward circled the little raft and kiwi waved, happy as a bird on the move. When asked just why he was sailing on a raft in the middle of the Pacific Ocean, the kiwi replied,

"Because, sir, I cannot fly."

The kiwi had decided to split the old island after a gang of bipeds had invaded. The sail feathers were all that was left of poor Dodo, who never had learned to move very fast. Kiwi asked Edward how far was the land of eucalyptus and koalas.

The Land of Eucalyptus and Koalas lay another two thousand miles distant.

"Slow but sure." said kiwi. "Steady on!" And with that he resumed his singing as Edward headed south.

As it became colder he felt her longing for the warm lands, but there was this other longing too, a longing for some uplifting moment that would transform her into something beyond what she was. This desire to step beyond that for which she was made resonated within Edward like a bell that echoed on and on. Soon, the ice floes below became numerous and he could see the astounding mountain heights of the southlands. Now, she seldom ventured from Edward's back and the insistent whisper breathed in him, "Hurry! Hurry! We are dying!"

The palace of Motta's father, the Snow King, arose in fabulous spires of blue-white between which glided long steamers of mist. Into the vaulted hall lined with massive polar bears, penguins and ice poppies the weary bird glided to give his charge.

"You have come a long way," Motta observed. "Need any special favors?"

Edward mentioned his friend kiwi, who at that moment was languishing becalmed in the middle of the wide Pacific with a broken E-string. Motta forthwith sent a gust to propel kiwi rapidly the rest of the way to New Zealand.

Now, it must be said that Motta did not exactly fall head over heals for an old randy king she had never seen. The truth of the matter was that, unknown to everybody, that unruly little boy, Eros, had fired one of his subversive arrows right though Motta as she had flown over the Seven Seas, Inc. She had seen Atlantis not just once, but many times as she had whistled over the waves, which conceal nothing from the eyes of a goddess as they do from the eyes of ordinary men. But of course, she was quite shy and not a little proud, being the daughter of a king and all, so she had never made the first move.

After Edward had given his message to her, she leaped up with joy and roared about the Antarctic at a great rate in her BWM (Bitching Wind Machine), dragging Edward along in the violence of her exuberant wake until there at the edge of Antarctica she cause not just a single ice crystal but a massive glacial chunk to go Whomp! right into the ocean, sending ripples all the way the boardroom of the Seven Seas Corporation.

The union of the two lovers was as passionate, sentimental, glorious and tediously trite as such meetings between gods and goddesses tend to be, hence we shall not pause to relate the raptures of Atlantis and Motta. Their relationship has been long lived. Periodically, as a kind of commemoration of that day, Motta sends another chunk of ice into the ocean.

This is why glaciers creep down to the ocean and break off.

Our concern is with Edward, who discovered among the general hoopla that his own companion had come loose from his back. He could feel her presence some where in the vast whiteness of Antarctica, but he could not, even with his superior eyes find her. She was all white against the snow. For a long time he crossed and recrossed the land of ice and snow without success, calling and calling but not finding her.

And so that just about brings us to the end of the story. In gratitude the newly merged corporation Sea-Wind renamed Edward as Albatross, which in the dualistic language of Parnassan means Bearer of Joy, or He Who Flaps But Little, or something like that. He was blessed by Motta, who put all the winds at his disposal, and by Atlantis, who put him under the special protection of the Seven Seas.

This is why the albatross sails so effortlessly on the wind for such incredible distances without ever touching land. Still today you can find the albatross in the lands of the south, sailing here and there, looking for his lost companion, bringing messages from Atlantis far and wide to every corner of His Corporation.

THE BROKER

Her name was Mary and she just graduated from Berkeley with a degree in English with an emphasis on medieval studies, the apple of her father's eye. Her hobbies were music and astronomy. Her parents had retired to a home in Mountain View, purchased after long years of careful garnering of the sheaves of a careful middle-class existence. After graduation she went to Europe with her boyfriend, somewhat to the displeasure of her father, but she had worked hard and had earned it. She was grown up and could do as she wished now.

Things went well until, on the sandy shore of Mykonos amidst the heavenly blue Aegean, she and her boyfriend broke up. While her boyfriend continued on the ferry to other islands, other places, another life apart from hers, she remained to piece her head together.

She rented a cabin to herself on credit and the luxury of living alone in a place of such beauty seduced her as no lover ever could. The weather held, the sand stretched far and away and the fabled wine-dark sea lapped gently against cliffs dotted with white-washed houses inhabited by a people she loved. At night she drank a lot of retsina and ouzo, sometimes with people she hardly knew, sometimes entirely alone. She was far from her father's machine-shop world where everything was so common and familiar. In the day, the sun beat down with hot indifference as she lay on the white sand, listless and uncaring. The future stretched boundless far and away.

Eventually, she pulled herself together and returned in high gear to find a job. First a job, then a life of her own as an independent adult. But the economy was bad. Everyone seemed in a bad mood. She could not find work in her field and the only office work offered her was that of a typist drone or a receptionist. Her typing was awful and she hated fielding phones for other people who always seemed to have plans. No one wanted an English major from Berkeley.

Out of desperation, she began sending resumes, making phone calls to almost anything that came up in the paper. On one of these group interviews, the man talked about working hard, doing 12 hour days, and steady growth in the company to phenomenal income. The man told her to come back for an hour long interview and some testing. She came back and was grilled on her ability to persist in a difficult field. She tested out very well. The next day she was called back and so she began her career as a stock broker trainee.

The year that followed was not a joke. She got up each morning at five o'clock, turned on the news, went down to the station and read the Wall Street Journal on the way to work. At seven, she came in the door and went to work with her mentor who instructed her by example. The work consisted of incessant telephone contact with people off of a list while standing by a computer screen. The mentor sold bonds and securities to individuals and selected groups over the phone, occasionally picking up a second phone to complete transactions with New York all day as long as the Borse was open. When the market closed in the East, the two of them continued for hours, selling over the phone those transactions that would complete the following day.

By seven in the evening, she would gather her study materials for her series licenses and would go to the library to study for her broker's exams until ten. Then she went home to toss a can of something into the pan to eat. This went on for over a year, six days a week. The selling, which generated commissions to her mentor, continued on Saturday. She remained on a stipend salary until the day she took her exams and passed. The stipend was enough to slow the amount of her debt, but not enough to actually cover all her living expenses, so when she got her license through sheer work volume, she celebrated with a couple people who had remained friends during the long apprenticeship. Now she could go to work and have a shot at earning her 80,000.

The next week, she went on to commission only and so she got herself a desk and a telephone and a computer screen.

It went slowly. But she had drive and energy. She knew that the field was tough. All the material had warned her it was tough, but she was not ready for the sheer volume of indifference. No one wanted to buy. The leads she got didn't seem to pan out at all. She got in at seven and worked the phones, really worked those phones until past seven at night. No luck. She couldn't understand how Al managed to do it. She said all the right things, but no one wanted to buy bonds from her. Either they already had a broker, or they just didn't want to buy. Some listened politely to her patter, even asked questions, but no luck. Days went by. Twelve hour days. Others seemed to be selling. Others, newcomers like herself, just did not come in after a while. She could see them looking around in confusion, wondering what was wrong, but she did not want to be like them. She could see Al over there and Nancy. Somehow they seemed to have gotten the knack. They were there and they made money. All it took was a start, a little juice. It could be done. She made a few nickle and dime sales, but not enough to even match the stipend she had received. The end of the month approached. Twelve hour days. All alone and the telephone. The white beach of Mykonos with the sun beating down so hot.

She was going crazy and she knew it. All it would take would be a single sale, just one or two with a thirty percent return. She knew the goddamn market and this was bull shit, utter bullshit. In desperation she started going through the phone book and cold calling at random. Then, by city district where she knew the money was. Cold cash out there, just lapping at the shore. Still no luck. She wondered when they would just throw her out for being so unproductive. She resolved to try harder.

The day came, one of those twelve hour days, when she had no one to call. She had no more resources, her rent was due, her cards gone to the limit in charges. A single can of beans waited at home for dinner. But she knew the market. She could see the millions flying by on the computer screen and she could make the call on the dime by the way it would go and she was always right. Most of the time.

No one who has not done sales, gone door to slammed door, stood like a fool in the middle of the showroom with nothing to show after eight hours of hell can imagine was it was like. And this was not eight hours, it was twelve hours a day, day in and day out six days a week in the company of men who owned four houses and fully paid Porsches in each garage.

Al gave her tips, suggested she try friends, family, people she had met a long time ago. Someone who would remember her, trust her in this most sharkish of businesses. But her friends had graduated from Berkeley too. They didn't have any money. Her associations all were blue-collar. No one had the kind of money it would take. Not all of her friends together.

She called her father. He was happy to hear from her, this his successful stockbroker daughter. She had told him nothing about how bad it was going, how far in she was, but he could tell. He could hear the call in his daughter's voice, the hidden cry. He didn't know much about the market, but he knew his daughter was in trouble. He got it out of her that she needed a buy, a big buy to pull her out of the hole. Her mind stopped working and that was the beginning of the end. He told her he would see what he could do. She felt her heart stop.

The rest of the day she tried indifferently well to sell, drifting on a loose current, an eddy of something that used to be emotion, but now was something else. She didn't know what it was. She couldn't collect a commission directly from a family member -- company rules -- but something could be worked out. Something could be worked out with Al.

When her father called, he had fifty thousand to invest. She didn't know where he had got that kind of money, didn't ask. She was now a well trained broker and she executed the transaction with Al efficiently and quickly. When the deal was done, she was out of the hole. She felt grateful to Al, and in gratitude she let him make love to her the day after.

He passed some leads to her after that, and some of these bought in low volume, as if testing the soundness of her. Some of her friends also came through with low volume investments. These she banked into state and municipals as the amounts were so low anyway. What mattered was that the ice had broken.

Tuesday, October 1989, dawned rosy and clear on what would be the second worst day of her life. She thought this was the worst thing that could ever happen when the market bottomed out that Black Tuesday, but the worst was yet to come. That day the phones slammed down louder than usual and the blatted expletives slung around the room like soft turds from sling shots as hundreds, thousands of people lost a collective 13 billion dollars in soft trades. No one jumped from any windows here -- everything was hermetically sealed, and unlike the traders themselves, who had been eaten by an immense and voracious bear, the sales people came out unmarked. Rueful, but unmarked by a single tooth of loss. Only for those with a conscience would there would be bad nights ahead.

The next day the market closed to stop the panic. Wall Street shut down and in brokerages across the country the phones muttered desultorily in half-hearted consolation. Everyone closed early. Al told her the final truth during a lunch at Montella's over eggplant and red pepper. Nobody makes any money selling, he told her. You take the small commissions and use what you know to make quick steal and run trades on the market every day. That's why the phones were always busy. Only people whose entire life had been in the business could succeed with few exceptions. At least at MPV. Everybody who survived had come from families who had been in the business for generations. They already had their connections built before they came in. That's how they could make their 80,000. The market fed off of people like herself who came in and fed dollars to the machine. Put somebody in the room with a phone long enough and they would find some cash somewhere to put in. That's the way it was. Sometimes they got lucky. Most did not. It had happened to her her and she was no exception. They all dropped out or did just what she did: tap a source.

He had lost millions in this and as soon as he could he was going to take a long trip to think things over. He suggested she do the same. There eddied a thick silence between them. The eggplant rested limp and greasy in expensive piles untouched. After a while they got up. He paid the bill and they went back upstairs. In a little while she did not see him anymore.

That night she stepped out on the platform of her rail station under a night of clear, dry-eyed stars. It had been a long time since she had looked up to name the old, familiar shapes she knew. She walked the little ramp down to the street and took the connecting bus as usual to her apartment complex. She opened the door to her apartment to find an old man standing there in her living-room. An old man wearing a tan dustcoat, holding his hat in his hand. At first she did not know who he was, this old man looking so frail as he stood in the middle of her apartment.

It was her father. The manager had recognized him and let him in. That began the worst day of her life. Seeing her father and knowing what it meant. The money had been borrowed using the house as collateral. Now the house would be foreclosed.

She had graduated from Berkeley with a degree in English with an emphasis on medieval studies. Once the entire world had opened out for her. Doors had opened all down a long endless corridor of choices. She had been the apple of her daddy's eye. As the elevator shushed open and she stepped out on the fourteenth floor she felt older and channeled into a single track. Over the past year she had been well-trained for every case and she knew already what she would do.

She asked to speak with the Manager of the House.

In an imaginary scene she confronts him as he is pissed at the panic, at the wreckage and the disorder at deals gone bad and the following mood which was going to surely twist sales into a frigid knot. In addition, he had lost a couple million and a house. Gone, just like that.

"You already have FOUR houses! You ASSHOLE!" She snaps at him. Then she really lets him have it: all of the past year and a half of frustration, of sacrifice of twelve and fourteen hour days at shit wages to benefit a slime bucket of fucking leeches who never produced anything useful in their lives.

But this is an imaginary scene. She is well trained now. She is professional. And she meets with the manager who consents to give her a salaried position as a broker's assistant. One with normal human hours and a relatively decent wage. A wage from which she can count on paying back what was owed. And she would stay in the field about which she had learned so much.

Her parents and she moved into a rental apartment in Daly City and her life became the mechanized hum of another world. Except that she kept her love of music. Every year the firm would host a seminar of new recruits after five and she would take care of the basic administration of the event. Afterwards, the young faces fresh out of college would gather in twos and threes in the plaza at the base of the high rises and talk about that magical 80,000 and the twelve hour days of training. She would go out then and walk among them, listening to their innocent talk, the talk of hopes and dreams without the dry-eyed awareness of reality. There would always be one there, with longish hair and an earring and a suit that somehow seemed inappropriate. This was the one who carried a little lost hope. "Look up", she'd say, standing next to a bench. And they'd look up at the towering perspective of the inward leaning buildings and higher up to the black openness where a ring reeled through a band of glittering dust -- the belt of the hunter chasing and being chased across the infinite pantheon of stars.

"They came in from the City of St. John without a dime." she'd say. And if he saw the animals then, then there would be one who would be saved. And this was the only extravagance that she allowed herself. Now she was careful, and it would take a long, long time to pay everything back that she owed. But little by little, she knew she would do it.

DANA & ALLEN

This story is about Dana and Allen. It is a simple story, but it must be told. If this story were not told, there would be nothing. It is their very own story -- the ecstasy of their dreams and the anguish of their chromosomes.

They first met in a hallway of Sterne, O'Neal, Ahkmatova and Knabbert, a firm which enjoys stretching itself intermittently from the 12th to the 36th floors of a downtown highrise at Stevenson Place in the City, but it was on the 15th floor that their story begins. On their first meeting, not much happened, really. They smiled at one another then passed on to their respective destinies.

Actually, they never would have met were it not for the most fortuitous of circumstances. Dana, who possessed at least two healthy X chromosomes in each one of her cells, worked on the 36th floor in the Contracts and Communications Department and Allen worked on the 9th floor in the mail room. Dana had come down to pick up a deposition from a client, a famous operatic tenor. Allen, possessor of the broken Y chromosome, was changing elevators to go to the 39th floor to enjoy his lunch.

It must be said here that Allen did not take his lunch on the 10th floor cafeteria because he was a snob or because he was anti-social. In fact, his broken chromosome enabled him to enjoy baseball discussions with his colleagues very much, although he did not understand the game and could never remember the difference between RBI and MBA. The reason he took the elevator to the 39th floor was that there, he could enjoy a view from the plate glass windows embracing the sail dotted Bay on one side and the ocean on the other while the range of high rises stood up all around and he could see people far below, like the parking lot attendant at First and Mission, whose saxophone glittered like an Australian tree-frog. Allen would stare for almost twenty minutes before unwrapping his sandwich, invariably a salami and cheese on french bread smeared with Dijon mustard. Today, however, he did not admire the view so much and he let his sandwich sit in his lap a long time in thought as he leaned against a concrete support pillar.

He stood up and pressed against the glass of the 39th floor speculating what it would be like to fall in endlessnessness. He wondered about the astounding talents of barn swallows. He pondered the illimitable nature of clouds and the relation of And he considered the multifarious ingredients of salami, the sum of which no one would ever know.

By a miracle of reflections and re-reflections, from the 39th floor to the 101 California Building to the fanlights of the Sheraton, over to that squat building off Market and down to the 36th and her very own window, as Allen reflected upon these things, Dana saw the image of a man hovering outside her cubicle. He stepped back, flying without wings, a man whose face wrote the book on despair and longing. A man with an agonized expression holding what looked to be a salami sandwich on french bread there 36 floors above the street.

She turned off her desk light, which brought the image into sharp focus and when she did that her image appeared to him. He looked surprised. He waved to her. Hello. The woman waved back. It seemed to him that an angel had appeared. Somewhere a door opened and just as suddenly as she had appeared, she was gone.

Allen was so excited he couldn't eat. This was really amazing! An angel had appeared. To him! At lunchtime at that! For the rest of the day, Allen moved in a state of exaltation and suspense such that not even the coarse comments of Jeff in the mail room could drag him back to earth again.

He went home in the same state of mind passing the sax player at First and Market with a light spring in his step, a wave and a greeting that pumped brilliance into at least a bar and a half.

Fifteen minutes later, Dana walked by and dropped a dollar into his cap, stood a moment with a perfectly beatific smile on her face and then passed on.

The next day, Allen rushed up to the 39th floor precisely at twelve and there she was, dressed in a long white dress, her chestnut hair not stirring a strand in what must have been a perfect hurricane outside the windows. At first she did not seem to see him at all, then she looked up as if pulling away from some profound contemplation.

On the 36th floor, Dana pushed the COBOL program aside and looked up for the fifteenth time that day to see her visitation had returned: a dark man standing in a silvered room. What was he? A scientist conducting an experiment? A theatrical projection from some hidden camera? Shyly, he offered her a sandwich. She smiled, shook her head, mouthed the words, "Who are you?"

Allen understood. But what a question! How could he explain something so complex without words? He shrugged, turned about. There was nothing up there in the empty floor to assist him other than elbow joints, exposed sub-flooring, wires and PVC worming along retainer walls. His arms went out, palms out, in universal sign of wordless futility. She approached the glass and brushed the surface with her fingertips. He responded in kind, the crystal seeming to vibrate in answer. He recognized her then as the dark-haired woman with whom he had shared smiles on the fifteenth floor a day ago.

Now, this moment of tenderness was far from private. In fact, all over downtown office workers, janitors, law clerks and secretaries had left their desks to stand before certain windows to observe two figures, a man and a woman hovering in space, soundless and without touching, trying to communicate and each responded according to his and her own need and temperament. The law clerks of 101 California all stared in wonder. The secretaries of Wilson, Sonney, Richman and Rosewater left their midday soaps to cluster in conversation. Two window washers, Ray and Sal, hanging on a platform before the great fanlights of the Hyatt paused in their work. "Paolo and Francesca!" shouted Ray, who was something of a medievalist. On the uncompleted top floors of the Rincon Annex steelworkers harnessed to immense H-beams whooped and hollered encouragement and made bets on the outcome. Many predicted a torrid romance. Others foresaw a terrible catastrophe of shattered glass followed by a tragic fall.

"Where are you?" mouthed Dana, who understood that Allen was neither a ghost nor a space-time traveler from another dimension.

Allen shrugged. He could tell the image was speaking to him, but he was no lip reader. This was not a time for complex negotiations. This was no time for elaboration. He mouthed back three words, the only words which could be unmistakable under the circumstances.

Not only did she understand, so did everyone else. The City went wild. The secretaries swooned, laughed, ran back to get coffee and return to order sandwiches delivered from the pizzeria on Mission and First. Ray looked at Sal and Sal looked at Ray and winked. The steel workers slapped each other on the back and did Irish jigs from one reinforced pillar to another. Hardened EMTs shoved back mirrored sunglasses, forgot their Y chromosome heritage and glad-handed fairy deadheads. Tie-dye shirts ran to embrace startled pinstripes. From deep within the black heart of the B of A Building messengers rushed down to the street to report the news to dispatchers sweltering in the enclosures of Steuart Street and Main. They broadcast the events to other messengers who dropped the news at law firms all over town and at least one proposal of marriage was accepted in an architectural firm by a deeply hennaed gal who received the mail from a leather jacketed lad who promised to tattoo her name on the only free patch of shaven skull left on him. As they exchanged earrings, the balloon lady sent up a bouquet of green, orange and white balloons.

Down on the grimy intersections of Market and Sixth, people suddenly stopped, looked up and noticed trees blooming in the plazas. At Halliday, where the old crazy man honks salvation through a dirty megaphone a thrash guitarist started playing "Europa". All of a sudden, everybody noticed it was Spring.

The close of the hour approached and Allen pointed at his watch. Time to go. One of the secretaries at 101 California grabbed a piece of cardboard and a large felt tip pen and after a moment pressed it up against the glass. Good job Josephine!

As a message on graven tablets this message floated out of the clouds to appear before Dana and Allen: "!kroW retfA teeM".

This galvanized the redoubtable and intelligent Dana, who pointed, gestured, and mouthed words while Allen scratched his head. The female figure gesticulated wildly, pointed at her open palm, mimed a clock, pointed to the earth while the entire City held its breath. Would he get it or would the legacy of the broken chromosome prevail, that unfortunate XX which becomes in the male a limp XY, causing half of the species to forgo understanding at least one half of the time and thereby leading to all sorts of dreadful confusions, obfuscations, battering of heads and nervous jumping up and down? He considered his sandwich bag, the clouds, Dijon mustard, the curvature of the earth, and thereby got it, as men usually do, by thinking about something else.

Meet here! Meet here! After five! Five! Five! Five!

He nodded. Five o'clock. He disappeared. Lunchtime over.

That day, bosses everywhere were astonished by a surge in productivity. Suddenly there was tons of work to be done. So much so that eager offers of overtime astounded the dour and jaded managers throughout downtown. Dana found reason to work late on her program which seemed to require meticulous debugging. Five passed and files of unsuspecting workers loosened ties, changed into decent sneakers and dropped down the elevator shafts to scatter into underground tubes, cafes and aerobics gyms, there to hear the most incredible stories of mysterious appearances, lights in the sky and at least three dozen scientific explanations for the Virgin of Guadalupe even as heated assignations took place impromptu and arranged between couples abruptly raging with unbridled desires. Even so all but a prelude for what was to come, as six o'clock passed without an appearance.

Lights began going out as the skyline took the flames of day into the dark arms of the sea. The bridges lit up with their usual arcs and the overtimers gave up one by one, in twos and threes switching off desk lamps and overheads with sighs and the jangling of evening keys. The late stayers went down the long, long elevators to the street to land there and look up, wondering at the wheel of stars above. They put off going back to bedroom communities of Pleasanton and Walnut Creek to chat over glasses of Chardonnay in Harringtons and the Saloon.

Meanwhile, Dana put aside her pen, switched off her terminal and shut down the lights to her office to observe the moon, dear sister, rising over the headlands. It was then that the moon, streaming silver into her dark office, as Dana stood with one hand upon the door, did the duty of the sun without having to combat the reflection defeating office lights.

She now could see him clearly, sitting with his back to a wall in what looked like a spaceship or some place out of this life entirely. The moon's image appeared as a huge disk over his shoulder. He held out his hand, palm outward, calm. How to mime the display of passion in this voiceless place. She placed her right hand over her heart. Her sense of caution overwhelmed, something hammering inside her to escape, she turned, grabbed a marker and wrote on a piece of computer paper, "Floor 36. Elevator. Now!" Before she could finish, someone knocked on her door. A male hand turned the knob, flooding the office with fluorescent light from the hallway.

It was Jeff, the accountant from down the hall, who had had a crush on her ever since he had broke up with that poodle from Contracts Management. His broken Y chromosome impelled him to ask if she was all right. Working late? What happened to the lights? It seemed he would talk on and on. He raised his hand, twisting slightly so as to let the light catch his Rolex. Need a ride? She stamped her foot so hard the heel on her left shoe broke off. He would not go. It was dangerous downtown this hour. Besides her shoe was broken. It was no use. It would have to wait until tomorrow. She resolved to do something absolutely awful to Brad.

Allen, saw only a door open and two figures fading out. Finally, he understood the nature of the image. He ran to the elevator and jab-jabbed the button. Ages later the left lift arrived and he zoomed down to the thirty-sixth, sprinted to the transfer elevators hopped impatiently from one foot to the other while he watched the right-hand elevator making its descent floor by floor, until the doors swished open, he hopped in and waited as the elevator leisurely tick-ticked to the ninth, where a janitor got in, pressed the hold switch brought on his barrel of implements and his vacuum, and, oh yes, the big bag, and finally released the hold switch. He got off on the eighth and Allen was on his way again. The cavernous lobby echoed with his footsteps. No one was there except for the security guard. Yes, someone just left, a man and woman. The woman was limping. They went that way. Allen, breathless, ran to the doors to view the streets across which nothing moved other than skittering bits of newspaper and old calendar pages.

The next day, while in the windowless mailroom, Jeff, his co-worker started in again about baseball and his sexual prowess. Jeff belonged to the sort of individual who does not possess the slightest amelioration for the broken chromosome. Many have learned to adapt to a certain absence; others have developed compensatory mechanisms, enabling the gender to survive. Jeff, at the age of thirty-eight found himself working in a mailroom and few are those who more than Jeff deserved to be there, for his great pleasure in life, probably greatest pleasure, was talking about his penis and where he liked to put it. He talked about it so much that Allen began to doubt the man possessed any other organs at all. This sunny Monday, Jeff wanted to know if Allen had "got any" last weekend. Hey, how about that dark-haired chick on the thirty-sixth floor. Hot, hot, hot. Heard she would go down at the drop of a hat . . . .

Allen surprised himself and Jeff with a rapid swing that was meant more as a, well, shot across the bow, if anything, but the terrible legacy of the broken chromosome worked itself out in this case. He still had a court stay in his hand at the time and, as Jeff staggered back against the mail-slots, he looked down at the crumpled document as if the paper had just sung to him a little song from La Traviata. The supervisor came in just then to see a furious Jeff splattering nose-blood all over the precious depositions in the cart and pointing at Allen. "Dhat guy'sh crayshee!"

Allen was summarily fired and escorted down the elevator by an armed guard to the outside doors where he looked about at the laughing couples on California Street, walking arm in arm to the brilliant chops of a distant saxophonist playing Coltrane. Everyone looked to be in a good mood; even the window-washers were singing to themselves, but Allen, who had left his salami sandwich in the fridge up above cursed his luck, wishing he had never ever smiled at the dark-haired woman on the fifteen floor.

47

SWITCH

He awoke trying to scream, but no voice came out as he gasped for air. He had asked the reason for his arrest, but no one would tell him. He lay on the cot hearing the blood inside his ears until the Observer came for him.

As they approached the Observation Chamber, the odor tightened Korol's abdomen and the Observer became more agitated, as he always did, like a man waking up on a sunny Monday morning before going to work. The Observers eyes began to dart back and forth and his right hand jangled the pens in his coat pocket.

They arrived before the door and as the Observer took out his keys to shift Korol's manacles from the back to the front, commenting as usual that this was necessary "to prevent damage", Korol looked down and noticed that the Observer, who otherwise dressed conservatively in a starched shirt, black pants, observation coat with many pockets and a clipboard, wore, instead of the standard black gunboats soft brown shoes with crepe soles.

Something about the Observer, perhaps his beard and his glassed, reminded Korol of a Talmudic scholar. Because of this, Korol decided to speak, and so, before going in, he commented to the Observer, "How precise. You have learned well from your masters."

The Observer halted and his eyes opened wide at this deviation from procedure. But his professionalism returned and he motioned Korol to enter. As he readied himself, an element of curiosity caused him to ask, "What do you mean by that?"

"The National Socialists of course."

They went in.

Afterward, Korol lay on the bench in his cell, staring at the ceiling a long time. After a time, the light slanting from the high window pointed to the crack where the spider lived and Korol slept. He dreamed again of his first conversation with the Observer, when he had asked the reason for being here and the Observer had replied that, since Korol had been imprisoned, he must therefore be guilty as the Tribunal is not permitted by law to err.

Inside the Chamber, at the next Observation, Korol turned and spoke to the Observer.

"Kishkes," said Korol, his voice resonating in the chamber.

The Observer looked up from his clipboard and their eyes met. "What did you say?"

"Reminds me of kishkes. This. My mother used that word."

The Observer made a note. "You must call me 'Doctor'," he said.

"Platkes. Did your mother make you platkes when you were little?"

The Observer did not look up, however his pen stopped moving. "You speak. You should not speak."

"All this time you people have been trying to get me to speak what you call the truth, is it not true? Hokay then. You are going to get an earful."

The Observer did not move. He could not. The positions for the interrogation had been fixed. A chain started winding on a drum and machinery began to move behind Korol.

"Kishkes," said Korol before adding in a rush, "Platkes. Knodel, chicken soup, cherry jam, twist-bread, maybe marzipan for something exotic after. And fire . . .".

"Stop it!" said the Observer.

Korol leaned his head back and said tiredly, "Why?" The distant dripping resonated. "My bube used to say when I was quite small, 'Well, just because you want to see what you want doesn't mean you gonna hear what you're gonna hear'."

"We can hurt you."

"My boy, I think we all know that by now." Then, Korol smiled at the face of the Observer. "What else you gonna do, hey? Any new versions of the parrot perch not tried before? Shocks, racks, fire . . .".

"I would not laugh in your position just right now."

"I know. But then, there's a little hope for you."
Korol sniffed. "What did you have for lunch before
coming over here?"

"I had an excellent ham sandwich. And a crab
salad. You see, I can eat anything I want."

"So can I." Korol laughed. "You are just like
me."

Thin lipped and stalking, the Observer brought
Korol back. Before reentering his cell, Korol said, "I
especially like the little honey my mother put on the
platkes."

The Observer slammed the door. "Your mind
is going. You are going crazy."

They began piping strange music continuously
into the cell at all hours, which halted periodically for
the sound of hysterical laughter before resuming.
This went on continuously for twenty four hours until
Korol, taking a comb and a piece of tissue began humming along. When the music stopped, he bowed as if
to a large audience.

The next time, a man wearing a bowler hat, a
long black frock coat and enormous black shoes
greeted them outside the Chamber. Two curls twirled
down to each side of his face and a large plastic nose
perched above a jovial beard. In his lapel, an enormous sunflower nodded to them.

The man's arm tensed and a stream of water
shot out from the sunflower hitting Korol in the face.
The Observer and the clown burst into uproarious
laughter. Korol went up to the clown and embraced
him, calling him a brother and said, "So you too are a
schlemiel!"

The clown choked and was throttled into a fit of silence.

After the observation, somewhat enlivened by the clown, who toyed with chains on the wall, spun the ratchets on the table and playfully set fire to spider's nests with coals from the brazier, Korol started chuckling to himself.

"Your mind is going," his companion observed.

"And a good thing too, at this point."

"Everything is taken from you. We can do anything we want," the Observer said.

"You know, I quite like you," said Korol. "You walk a little like my Uncle Sirin. He was a good man and made excellent preserves."

"You, you walk like an old man, bent and broken," said the Observer. "You are getting old and senile. Dementia, it is."

Korol patted him on the arm, jangling his manacles as he did so. "It's all right.   I'm sure you're a good boy. Perhaps I am an old man. Forgetting things." He went into his cell, and said, "Yes, how could I forget. It was sugar she put on the platkes. Not honey."

He expected the door to slam, and when it did not, he turned to see none other than the Director standing there outside the door, looking not at him, but at the Observer.

That night, there were no more broadcasts into his cell. In the morning, instead of the usual thin, cold gruel his meal came hot, with eggs, potato pancakes, jam, a cup of coffee. Later that afternoon, instead of the Observer, a guard appeared to march him to the Official Privy. The guard did not comment about Korol's sex life or make any comments at all, in fact.

That afternoon, the Director came bouncing into the cell, followed by not less than two secretaries, three administrative assistants, four uniformed guards with badges and tassels and two deputies carrying numerous government writs, official seals, and maces indicating high degree of officialness. The Observer slipped in behind and stayed close to the wall.

"How ARE you my good man!" shouted the Director.

Korol nodded.

"My good sir, esteemed Prisoner, today is a fortunate day. Are you aware of that? The Director extended his hand to one side and received scroll tied with red ribbon from an A.A. "Today is your lucky day! Today your most longed for wishes, your deepest desires are to be granted by the magnaminiousness of the State and the power invested in me. I am sure you are aware we have been watching you closely, very closely and the Highest Royal Tribunal has determined that you are ready. Now, now, no need to weep for joy. Time for weeping later. My glasses Please! Thank you. Ahem!" The director adjusted his reading glasses above his stout cheeks and unrolled the scroll to read in a loud declaiming voice," Esteemed Prisoner, Honored Guest of the State, it is with great pleasure we, the Highest Royal Tribunal hereby announce that on Monday following at 9:00 am, GMT, the exact nature and details of the crime which you have committed and found guilty, in absenteeum, shall be announced to you and the assembled Assembly without exception or delay. The Ceremony has been fixed. I say," he said, looking over his glasses all smiles and rising up on his toes, "Is that not perfectly delightful! All shall be revealed! The sight of your tribulations is at hand!" The assembled collection of secretaries, assistants and guards applauded, all smiles, with the exception of the Observer, who looked absolutely wretched.

Someone in the corridor tooted on a trumpet.

The Director raised his hand to bring silence. "But there is more. Listen! Ahem! Subsequent to the reading of the charges and judgment of the Most High Tribunal, the Esteemed Prisoner is to be brought to the central Square with the space of 30 minutes, without exception, and there at precisely 9:35 is to be hung by the neck until thoroughly dead!"

The Director removed his glasses, beaming. "Is this not wonderful! The stars have smiled upon you at last. Your deepest wishes amid trial of rack and fire. Congratulations! My good man, please allow me to shake your hand if it has not been broken, ah, good! Marvelous! Excellent health still! The cuisine has not disappointed you I hope? This is a happy day. Here, one of my cigars . . .".

There followed an extended scene of cigar smoking and sipping brandy from large snifters while flashbulbs of the press went off and with the Director chattering constantly in high spirits he posed with Korol, the guards, his staff and with a pretty blond secretary.

Before going, the Observer edged up to Korol and hissed, "If you had not spoken, this would not have happened. It could have gone on forever, but you didn't play the game.

The days to Monday slipped by without event or visitation. The Bible, the Torah, the Koran, and a copy of a tract by L. Ron Hubbard were left at Korol's disposal.

On Sunday, the Observer dropped by for a visit. His face looked pale and his eyes deep set and hollow. "I am condemned," he said on entering. "Everything is finished. How can you sit there? Don't you have any feelings?"

"Actually I feel indifferent."

The Observer took a step back. "Indif.... But what about me!"

Korol tugged on his chin gazing idly up to where the squat observation camera blinked it's cold little eye. "It appears you are progressing nicely."

The Observer left in a huff.

Monday morning, breakfast arrived promptly at 7:00. At 7:25 they came for him, responding to his protest against the hasty hour that there must be ceremony to be observed first and everything had been fixed.

The Most High Tribunal sat behind a big oak table in the Judgment room. Each one of them wore tuxedos and on each one of their heads party hats made of cardboard perched astride their wigs. The Chief Justice used a noisemaker to bring the court to order.

"Esteemed prisoner," he began, and as he read the charges, written entirely in a mixture of Latin, Greek and Catalan, with which he had some pronunciation trouble, his speech was punctuated by cheers from the gathered throng. Confetti flew through the air, balloons were popped and a huge banner gilt with stars and Korol's name dropped from the rafters at the final verdict. The secretaries all wore bridal gowns and the guards wore green tuxedos. A waiter scurried about with a tray of canapes and champagne as things wound up. A toast was drunk to the health of the Prime Minister. Then to the jury. Then to the armed forces. The warden asked Korol if he would offer a toast, and Korol, quite caught up, honored his esteemed Observer and the splendid prison security system. This started another round of toasts to the judges, the executioner, the bricklayers of the commonwealth, their mothers, motherhood, and finally a jovial toast was offered to the prisoner's health. By the time they left the chamber, the Chief Justice and the Warden were both red-faced and walking with the help of administrative assistants.

As they went into the square, packed with visiting dignitaries, the press, TV. cameras, curious onlookers and others besides, he looked up to see, just above the scaffold, the Great Clock ticking away the hours, just past 9:38.

There ensued a brief hiatus as the ribbon to the scaffold steps was cut with a pair of bronze shears and then they started going up with the Director guffawing loudly at a joke make by one of the ambassadors.

"Come along my good man, or you'll be late for the dance!" said the Director. Korol, still looking at the Great Clock, idly said, "I must be already dead. It's too late already."

An hush stunned the crowd into an acre of silence.

"What? What is it?"

"I only mean its 9:40." Korol said. "You've kept Mr. Death waiting five minutes already."

The black-hooded executioner glowered down at them, then bent to look at his own wristwatch, then up at the Great Clock in the campanile.

"What is this?" An ambassador said. "Let's hurry up. I have a luncheon with the minster of Andorra."

The Director flew into a rage, tossing his head back violently; so much so that his glasses dropped from his pocket and in the crush on the stairs, a clumsy Assistant stepped on them. The Judges began to approach.

"Idiot!" screamed the Director.

The Official Physician descended the stairs, picked up the pieces of the Director's glasses and handed them to him, whereupon the Director burst into tears. "No one would have noticed. You have ruined everything!"

"We can still get on with it," offered Korol.

The Imperial Judge came down from the stage as the restive crowd shifted its feet, complained, began to leave. "We have a problem." One of the pressmen looked up at the Great Clock and snapped shut his memo book. The photographer disengaged his flash attachment and put his things into his carryall.

"The time for the execution is inflexible. The ceremony cannot be changed." said the Judge.

The Director wrung his hands. "Not in all my twenty years . . . I shall never live it down. I am ruined. It's finished . . .".

The Judge cleared his throat. "This is grave."

Korol, feeling a little flippant, said, "For a dead man, I feel pretty good. Perhaps you can kill me again on another day."

The Judge cleared his throat. "Silence before the Omnipotent Law." He turned to the physician. "Can you do something here?"

"Well, hmm. As the time is fixed, and the time is past and no one can change time within the strictures of science and law, and as the ceremony cannot be changed, and additionally, in my professional opinion, no mortal being can survive a 10 foot drop with a rope about his neck, the Esteemed Prisoner must perforce by all the laws of medicine be at this time, dead."

The Director burst into action. "Then please sign this affidavit attesting to the proper condition of the formerly esteemed Prisoner. Thank you. Just a couple more forms here. Mr. Executioner . . . . Thank you. Man! That was close." He seemed not to see Korol any longer.

The Judge descended the scaffold to deliver his Speech of Conclusion to the dispersing crowd and the TV. technicians loading equipment into their vans, ending with, "The miserable wretch judged in proper form and ceremony and fully attested is declared to be lawfully executed as of 9:35 and is therefore dead as of 9:45 am, sans habemo corpus - I think that's the declination. Thank you. Go in peace and lawful respect of the powers that be. Mighty is the arm of our State.

The Observer appeared beside Korol, who had descended to the ground with the others by this point. "I would suggest we disappear before you are thrust into the bureaucracy of entombment."

Korol and the Observer walked through the indifferent mill of people, arm in arm, and with a flash of the Observer's badge, they exited the gates of the Prison among a throng of released prisoners, all very Esteemed and very much happy. The Director, who had become a bit unhinged at the days events, had released each one of them, saying that there must be no exceptions. Pale faces which had not seen the light of day for four years and more appeared blinking in the delightful sunshine.

In singles, in twos and in threes, the dead descended the little hill to walk again among the streets. A band of musicians started playing on the street-corner as the taboo against music was lifted. The Imperial Judges announced a festival of renewal while they thought these things over and the City once again filled with song and images of delight.

THE LAST ELIGIBLE BACHELOR IN SAN FRANCISCO

Ely had a problem. Strolling down Valencia on a sunny day he looked into the Cafe Club and who should he see but Vicki, Miriam and Donna all sitting together discussing the lack of eligible bachelors for their matchmaking service, "Elegant Eligibles". Miriam looked up just at that moment and grabbed Vicki's arm. As Miriam unfolded her lanky body upwards, Ely spun on his heel. He was already across the street and zipping down 20th by the time Miriam had started her loping gait out the door, followed by the quick Vicki with Donna barreling after. He looked over his shoulder and glimpsed the long legs of Miriam bounding across Valencia dodging through squealing traffic. Some vatro started screaming at her as the shorter Vicki twisted and turned like a linebacker through the line of cars.

Ely cut down Bartlett past the rows of stoops hosting women, boys, kids all turning to stare at the crazy white man now running full tilt with his coat flapping to either side.

This business about social control had gone overboard. Somewhere in the MENSA thinktanks, a retort had bubbled over while the lab tech had gone to lunch. The stuff had slopped all over the Urban Planner reports causing untold confusion during those late night meetings of the Illuminati of San Francisco deep beneath the bowels of the Mechanics Institute.

Undesirables were now making babies like grunions and the intelligentsia was threatened by a tidal wave of blathering babies destined for NASCAR and Monster Truck rallies instead of the Symphony.

Now an unholy mess existed and the decision to fix it was to make sure that every single male with the correct genome structure got properly mated; so the machinery had been put into place to complete the Grand Design.

Ely, for his part, after the last disaster with Diane, would have no part of it. His refusal to inseminate was emphatic. The threats of the Social Engineers equally so. Now, Ely was a desperate man on the run.

On Mission, Ely ducked into the Grilla Suiza and headed for the back when he was stopped by a boy wearing a server's apron. "Hey! Toilets for customers only!"

"Oh, oh. Gimme a taco."

"You want a regular or a special. Chicken, beef, special fish . . .".

"Gimmee a special fish. Everything in there."

"Hokay. It's not your ordinary taco."

As the boy took his order to the kitchen, he heard Donna's deep-voiced roar calling someone a son of a bitch. He got his taco, with hot sauce, paid for it and went immediately to the bathroom. There were bars over the window. He put the taco in his breast pocket and came out. The kid looked at him with an open stare.

"You got a back door? INS, abogado, senoras, mucho trouble. . . .

The boy looked at him. "I was born here, dude. You lose your English or what?", but he turned and led Ely past stacks of cans and tortillas to a door which the kid unlocked. The boy handed him a Jalisco -- tangerine flavor -- and wished him luck. Ely stepped into a small area filled with trash cans and empty crates, surrounded with a ten foot high wooden fence. The boy closed and locked the door.

Putting the Jalisco in his hip pocket, Ely stepped up onto one of the lidded cans and grabbed the top of the fence. The can tipped over. He hauled himself up until he could see the yard on the other side. A woman hanging out the wash looked at him and shouted as a pit bull bounded across the yard and put its forepaws up on the fence. Flecks of spittle flew to either side as the beast roared from a deep, red-mouthed rage. Ely moved hand over hand to the corner, pulled himself over and flopped into a mulch pile. On the other side of a chain-link fence the woman and the dog made much noise.

The houses came close together here, so he climbed over a low fence into the next yard and then into the next until he found a passage that let out into the street. Someone opened a window and started shouting at him in Spanish. He climbed over the gate and found himself on San Carlos Street. He ambled down to 19th where a low-slung Chevy, fire-engine red, pulled over facing the wrong way a few feet behind him. The doors opened and guys stared getting out of the car, two with baseball bats. Ely bolted down 18th to Mission, followed by the gang. On Mission he ducked into the first doorway that stood open. Guitars, clarinets and tubas hung from racks next to VCR's, turntables and an impressive array of candelabras and yarmulkes. "I wanna buy a fantod!" Ely shouted. Several helpers converged on him with the owner leading the way. "I got a fender strat, just came in and hardly used. For you only three-fifty. Make an offer."

The homeboys stood in a salt and pepper gaggle outside until one of them stepped in with his bat. The proprietor reached behind the counter and pulled out a huge rifle. "Outta my place. No trouble!" The homeboy squared his baseball cap and retreated.

"Damn emigrant!" he shouted. They left. Ely shifted his Jalisco from the pocket on his left to the pocket on his right. Then took it out and opened the bottle. He indicated the candelabras. "You Jewish?"

"Catolica," said the shopowner, aggrieved. "Everybody says we must be Jewish. A guy's gotta make a living. That coat is nice. You do something wrong?"

"Just taking a walk, dude. You see three women go by in a hurry? One a red head . . .?"

"Un Rubio?" said his assistant, a small man wearing penny loafers and no socks. "Si. Un Rubio. Mucho grande hermosa!"

"With a blond and a brunette?"

"Tres hermosas, si! You take their money?"

"No, no," Ely put his hands out in denial. He groped for a phrase of Spanish, a shallow swimmer in a deep river. "Passion."

The broker was only slightly sympathetic. "My friend, you must learn to govern your instincts. The male of the species is a ferocious sex-driven beast exceeded in appetite only by the female. Yet I understand. I give you two fifty for the jacket."

Ely shook his head. "I'm in a state of denial."

The broker turned his back.

The clerk leaned over to him. "You a Mason?" He pointed at the large capital "G" still legible on his sweatshirt from Georgia Tech. Ely shrugged.

The clerk told him that the Masons had to stick to one another in these difficult times. He pressed something into Ely's hand. "Take this as a token, amigo. Now go before the boss sees. He's a Forester."

Ely stepped out of the shop. The clerk had put a tiny camera into his hand. He slung the strap around his neck and walked toward the BART Station, taking hits off of his soda pop.

A gypsy fortune-teller stood up from her crystal ball to bar his path across the plaza toward the Bart Station. "A fortune for very little and some advice . . . ". She grabbed his arm.

He flapped his arm a bit, but she fixed him with a fixed stare. "I know the past, the present, the future and the mind of Our Mother the Holy Cow. You are being chased by three fates is not true?"

Ely gave her a dollar and the woman sighed. "Times are hard. The three fates are very close. I see woman trouble in your past and present young man. Gimmee a ten spot and I will tell you how you may escape." Ely hesitated. "The fury of woman scorned is not to be sneezed at lightly." Ely have her a crumpled mass of ones, which disappeared as if by magic. She then drew out a blue nylon cape stitched with constellations which she draped over his shoulders. She took a yellow mop from a shopping bag and placed this upon his head -- it was a wig with a plastic crown attached. She motioned for him to straighten his head gear, and as he did so, the gypsy did a kind of primitive rhumba in a circle about him, tossing star-shaped confetti on his head and shoulders. As she did this, she sang in a quavering voice a fair amount of gibberish about banishing vile spirits and so on.

Behind him he heard a familiar voice. "No one's seen him or everybody's seen him." It was Vicki.

"He's disappeared like magic, the son of a bitch." It was Donna. "He doesn't have the fucking right to get away single."

"Lard save us in butter; it's the times, the times. That ladies use such language in the street," said the gypsy.

"Hey you seen an asshole without a ring go by here?" Vicki asked the gypsy, who responded by offering to tell a fortune in cards for twenty bucks.

Ely moved toward the Bart entrance.

"Hey! My wig!"

Ely darted around the concrete barrier and down the stairs, leaping four steps at a time, cape flying and stardust cascading. Behind him, he heard Miriam's voice booming over the patter of Donna and Vicki and the gypsy. Ely hit the esplanade running, followed by his Jalisco which smashed into slick smithereens on the tile. He fired a quarter into the hat of the violinist in leather drag at the pillar before diving at the turnstile with his fastpass. Vicki landed into the slick and skidded into Miriam, going down for three as Ely had his card into the machine and out before the violinist could finish a single bar of Brahms. Ely trailed by a cloud of confetti stars rifled down the stairs.

Donna and Vicki and the gypsy scrambled to the ticket machine while Miriam simply tried to vault over the gate, but a guard aroused by the commotion met her before the stairs with his handcuffs, muttering about fare evaders.

The violinist adjusted his fishnet stockings and ambled in a loose-jointed way over to the gate to check out the scene. "Freaky, man!" He followed Donna and Vicki through the turnstiles past the prostrate Miriam.

Down on the platform, the three of them trolled along both sides. "Follow the stars," advised the gypsy.

Back up on the esplanade, Ely stepped out of the handicapped elevator and jog trotted toward the gate. Straight into Miriam and the security guard. "Hold it!" Miriam said.

Ely quickly whipped out his taco and held it to his head. "Don't come any closer. This is no ordinary taco!"

The guard pulled out his gun. Miriam, Ely, the taco, froze. Miriam's reddish profusion of curls tumbled in disarray over the shoulders of her black silk blouse. Her lipstick smeared to one side of her face and she sported a charming bruise on her elegant left cheekbone. One eye contact had leapt out, causing her to squint. Her wrists were cuffed together becomingly by a set of steel come-alongs. Never had she looked so ravishing.

"What have you done to your hair?" Miriam said.

Ely's throat constricted. He remembered the night of the full moon rhumba and the terra-cotta fish. From the open portal of the stairwell, bordered by stone images of Quetzalcoatl and Xanthippe, a golden light as of fresh brewed anchor steam streamed golden into the mezzanine. The distant sound of capoeira drums throbbed in the air. Life was still sweet. He edged sideways.

"Chill, dude!" said the guard, his gun menacing. Big gun, big bullets.

"Don't shoot him, idiot! He's got a job!" shouted Miriam. She swung her arms and jabbed the guard in the breadbasket. Ely tossed the taco, with the powdered cheese and hot sauce splattering into the guard's face and ran for the turnstile followed by

Miriam, who stumbled and grabbed at his head as he stepped through, leaving her with the wig in her startled fingers. As he bounded up the stairs, he could hear her screaming. The guard had got her with a flying tackle. As Donna came tearing up the downward escalator he turned and knipsed the camera, blasting the passage with strobe light before leaping up onto Mission.

Sprinting up toward the 16th street station he passed a matronly group of ladies who said to him as he passed, "Move to San Jose!" He jumped into an express jitney and the driver took off as Vicki came running up with a can of pepper spray in one hand and a set of handcuffs in the other.

"Full up!" shouted the driver, and they took off down Mission. "Home, home on the range!" sang the driver.

Much later Eli heard from a friend that Miriam and the security guard named Bob, had moved in together after a glorious mock wedding held on Mount Tam, where the violinist played Wagner's Lohengrin. Vicki and the gypsy started a business exporting used Levi's to Ireland and to Russia. Donna became a stripper for the O'Farrell's before opening a tattoo parlor for sailors, and was looking for a place to live in Pacific Heights as a wise maid while Elegant Eligibles languished without succor.

THE ANGEL

I am not Tabata. I am not here.
Do not pay attention to me or I hit you.
You must try to respond.
Sensei Tabata

On the 21st of February, between two parked cars on a cold night, someone raped Layla. He grabbed her as she was walking from an open poetry reading in the Mission near the Retlaw Camera Shop. He pulled her coat down to pin her arms, held a knife to her and ripped her dress to shreds. He threw her down then stamped on her right hand, breaking several bones. As soon as he was on top of her she felt powerless -- it happened so fast -- and so she did nothing. He told her he would kill her and he punched her in the face several times. He wiped himself with her underwear, called her a stupid bitch, and threw them on her face and then left her under the stars.

She lost her ability to concentrate at work, her attention span decreased, she forgot things, and she became irritable, exchanging sharp words with several colleagues which divided the office into fractious units to the point that the entire department began to slow down. She told people that she had hurt her hand in a ski slope accident. Some people said she was bitchy, had to be going through menopause, and she treated them with icy contempt. Eventually, she was let go. Although she had a masters degree from a prestigious university, she found no one would hire her, and so she found herself barely getting by doing the humiliating work of an office temporary, where the cold professional exterior she now cultivated became an asset. She stopped going to her assertiveness training, which she felt was a joke, and no one made her go back.

The few friends she told about the attack gave the support they thought she needed. Sharon brought her chicken soup on the weekends, and did some of the cleaning in the apartment that needed to be done -- as Layla, who used to like everything tidy, now let go until there were dishes in the sink, unwashed windows and science projects in the fridge. Sissy got her to go to a therapist she knew of, and the therapist, who was a man, listened sympathetically to the tales of things that never seemed to go right these days.

The therapist realized that this was an opportunity to get at archival issues that predated this recent trauma, and so Layla talked on through the hour. Afterward she felt a little better. The therapist sent her to an Awareness group, where Layla learned about things the group leader suggested that drew on attacks.

She learned about Denial and Anger and all the Stages and went through them all and then again. And again. And again, but somehow never getting to Acceptance. Someone told her she needed to accept Jesus as her Higher Power. Resignation, that she could accept.

She began to learn conscious urban survival skills. She stopped going out late, learned to walk a certain way, and began to choose her streets carefully. Light was her ally, darkness her enemy.

But she still had trouble getting to sleep at night. Her social life shrank to the circle of friends she had known well, she stopped going to poetry gatherings, and her relationships with men became tenuous. She went out with her close friends, tried dating again, but nothing seemed to last very long, and all the men seemed insipid to her. She did not hate men, in particular, just found most of them contemptible somehow, distant and not very appealing. She gradually stopped trying at all. Her friends understood. She kept a few male friends with whom she was able to talk in a distant way. No one pressured her.

A year went by. And then another. Her hand recovered, although she still felt some minor pain on rainy days. She still had times when she would lie in bed awake and cry to herself. She realized that her entire life had changed, that she had joined one third of the female population in a common experience. Someone told her she had come out of it pretty lucky compared to some. She lost a lot of weight, not having the energy these days to fix the complicated stuff she no longer enjoyed anyway, and although people complimented her on her looks, she felt that she looked older, lined. To keep hold of her precious fifteen minute breaks, she started smoking with the other temps on the street, and the cigarettes made her eyes look puffy, ugly in fact. She didn't have the energy to get out the old Singer either, and as things wore out, she replaced them with thrift shop bargains. On slow months, she lived off her credit cards, which never got canceled somehow, no matter how much she owed.

It was a life to which she found herself getting used.

On a sunny day weekend Diana breezed back into her life. Diana, wearing her bandanna and her halter strode back and forth in her kitchen, having just returned from Europe where she had been photo-documenting the breakup of the old Warsaw pact for a news magazine. But instead of talking about the exciting things she had been doing and seeing, instead of talking about the new series of affairs she had had with extraordinary men and women, she blurted, "What is with you, Layla? You look like hell. Your place stinks of cigarette smoke."

Diana had not heard the news and so Layla told her about the attack. She said that ever since then, she felt at a loss. She felt she couldn't go on this way. Layla expected a predictable response from Diana: a sympathetic ear and a diatribe about men. "What are you going to do now?" Diana said with an understanding voice.

"I don't know."

Diana told her to stand up, and Layla just shook her head, said she was tired. Instead of leaning against the fridge and uttering words of compassionate encouragement to make her feel better as so many of her friends had done, Diana grabbed her roughly by the arm and hauled Layla up and shoved her against the cupboard.

"It's three years now and look at you!" The air in the kitchen rang like a bell. "Fight back!"

Layla felt confused, uncertain how to respond. Her friend had always been intense, but she did not know how to react to this burst of energy directed at her. She said she couldn't do anything at all.

"Bullshit!" exploded Diana. "Get him out! Get free of it." Layla still did not know how to respond. "Fight!" Shouted Diana. She took the package of cigarettes off of the kitchen table and ground it between her palms until loose shreds of tobacco fell from the crumpled mess. "I am NOT going to sit back and watch you die. You were a manager for a corporation goddamn it. Now look at you!"

Eventually Diana calmed down. Somewhat. Then began Diana's program. Which Layla, in the torrent of Diana's energy, allowed to sweep her to art workshops and lectures by journalists, authors and healers. There she met others like herself, and besides the bonding that took place, she began to see how there were two ways to go.

Next, Diana got her a cat. This was not a nice cuddle muffin to keep the lap warm at night. This was a pure-bred Siamese kitten with the temper of Ghengis Khan. The first thing the animal did was to spray every table leg and chair in the house. The next thing it did was to destroy her sofa. One morning Layla woke up to see Khan sunning himself next to pieces of what had been the right hand armrest. It did not seem possible that something so small could have acted with such ferocity overnight. Layla got on the phone to Diana and demanded to know where she had gotten this thing. Diana told her it didn't matter -- the animal shelter -- just teach him who is boss. Layla told her she'd rather get rid of it. Out of the corner of her eye she saw something fling through space. It had jumped to the mantel. She turned to watch it stroll past the vase, which wobbled, toppled and fell to the flags in front of the fireplace, following which the creature began tearing at the bonsai plant set in the middle. "I hear something crashing," said Diana. "I think you had better do something about it."

The animal did provide a distraction.

The next thing Diana got her was a used personal computer. She got Layla to sit down every night to learn a spreadsheet program. "Just do it," Diana said, and left her. After a week, Layla went to her agency and demanded a better assignment using her new skill. The agent looked at her dubiously, but she tested well and the next day she got an assignment earning one and a half times more than what she had been getting. To celebrate, she treated Diana to dinner at Skates beside the Bay. Diana told her she was looking much better. "Have you been gardening? Where'd you get those nasty cuts on your arms?"

"Cat training."

At every opportunity Diana leapt on her, prodded her, goaded her, dragged her to black-belt basements hung with huge pictures of Malcom X and Rosa Parks where the voices of those who would not be put down shouted, provoked, asserted and refused to bow down. In a thousand ways Diana kept her running, active, awake, and challenged so that the stuff that was in her could come out.

Once again propelled by Diana, she went back to the assertiveness classes, and signed up for a management seminar. At the seminar she met men who seemed directed, open, non-vacillating and they treated her as an equal. In her new job, people began to treat her with respect. The department head came over to her one day and told Layla that it seemed she was vastly overqualified for the position she held and that she should keep her eyes open for permanent possibilities within the company.

Instead of going right home after work, largely to avoid facing Diana on her doorstep, she started going to a coffee shop she knew of near the office. There she sat and drank coffee while reading the paper until the traffic cleared on the busy freeways and surface streets. On the bulletin boards she noticed an ad for music lessons and she copied the number down. When she called later, a woman answered. The woman asked her what instrument she would like to play. Quite spontaneously, Layla said she wanted to learn how to play the flute. The woman said she didn't know much about the flute. Would the saxophone do? Layla said yes and the two of them arranged to meet.

Layla never learned how to play the saxophone, but she found that in the few lessons she took, her ear opened out to take in sound which always had been frightening noise to her. The enthusiasm of her teacher infected her with its passion for coding noise into harmony. All sounds of the city: horns, tires, construction, shouts, conversations in passing, blended into a piece of music that followed her everywhere she went. Sudden noises became the exiting percussion to her day. She also found that she had to quite smoking to gain enough wind to play more than a few bars.

She began to take notice around her. Look at other people, the way they were dressed, the way they interacted with one another. She noticed a mail-clerk, a young man in his thirties, who brought the trolley around twice a day to all the departments. No one paid him any notice; he did not call attention to himself. She overheard him talking to one of the secretaries, telling her about an exhibition he had seen over the weekend. He was a painter. The typist mentioned another exhibition going for a limited run, and the young man became quite excited, but it turned out he could not afford to go; they did not pay him enough in the mailroom to afford extravagances.

She began to keep tabs on him, where he was in the building, what he did, the kinds of places he went for his thirty minute break. Once, she watched him for an hour unloading a truck at the dock, his shirt off. He bent over once, close to where she sat, and she could see that he had a bright colored animal tattoo on his chest. But he stood up before she could identify what it was.

Layla resolved to do something for him. First she found out where he lived -- a single room studio on the third floor of an old Edwardian building in a district of town which had been forgotten by the developers and everyone else except for nightshift workers, waiters, painters, and would-be writers struggling to master their crafts -- and then she scoped out the hangouts in his neighborhood. At first she felt a like a voyeur, but she quieted herself with the thought that she was going to do something for this person she considered her own discovery.

In her own job hunt she had learned a lot about who was hiring what. She called Sissy, who worked in an architectural firm. She told Sissy that she had a friend who needed a favor. Next, she had to get her painter somehow to go over to the architect's firm. But she did not want him to know; she wanted to be in control, behind the scenes. There was a man who worked in the accounting department who often had spoken to her, trying to start a conversation, but she had given him the brush off. She went over to his desk and asked him what he was doing Friday night. He looked up from his computer screen and blinked at her a moment before the words registered.

His name was Brad.

They met at a bar around the corner and she let him take her home in his rattling Volvo to his studio. The accountant's apartment was sprinkled with little, hand-made ceramic animals, so she let him make love to her. It was the first time since the attack. When he was finished moving above her, and they rested side by side she mentioned that she had a friend in need of a job and could she ask a favor.

Monday, the accountant gave her a high sign. That afternoon, the mail-clerk came around with his trolley, absently dropping the mail into the in-baskets. Tuesday, the mail-clerk did not deliver the morning mail, but when he came by in the afternoon, he had a big smile and he walked as if wings had grown from his ankles overnight. Within a week, her painter was gone, working for the architect's firm at double the pay, according to Sissy who thought that this boy must be a new lover.

Meanwhile, the accountant, had stopped by her desk to tell her that certain internal transfers he had handled seemed to indicate that there would be a power struggle within a certain department. He let her know what that department was and that perhaps she could make use of the information.

Within the next week, a senior executive was ousted from the department mentioned by Brad. Someone else moved into his office. A vacated office stood open and ready and Layla took her chance by requesting an interview with the President through his AA, Mira. During her interview she told the President what her past professional experience had been, what she was qualified for, and what she thought she could do to improve the department. And smooth out any problems that might or might not exist between factions. She had experience and she had ability.

The next day, she got the job. By the end of the week, she was hanging a photograph of Khan sleeping peacefully next to her bonsai plant in her new office.

With her new position and increased salary, she was now able to accomplish much more. She contacted acquaintances she had met in the course of her temp jobs, who, like herself, had been languishing in underpaid situations and she got them hired into her department, which soon became the productive envy of everyone else. She took the large Christmas bonus the grateful president gave to her and contributed the majority to a local, struggling theater company, of which she had heard through her saxophone teacher.

She continued to go to her coffeehouse after work, but her schedule now included gallery openings featuring the work of the city's most interesting artists. At "her" painter's opening, which she made sure was well attended, she took the risk of buying one of his works and so held her first conversation with the man's life she had helped determine. His work consisted of a variety of semi-abstract tableaux culled from mythology. He was young, and still in search of his final style, but everyone agreed that he would do well with time and luck.

One of his works looked particularly appropriate: The painting she purchased depicted a shaggy hunter with the goddess Artemis. The artist had caught her in the moment of tossing his form into the heavens, his belt flaming up into a circle of stars. The symbolism to Layla was personal, and she did not tell the painter anything of her part in his development, but she hung the piece in a prominent place in her livingroom. She remained on good terms with her accountant, whom she matched up with one of the girls she had hired on. In the spring, Brad and the girl were married and Layla was invited to the wedding. Soon Layla found herself heading a small clan of people indebted to her for favors, and they would come to her office for advice and assistance. The past three years of her life became nothing but a butterfly dream, something that had blown away in a strong wind. She went to her cafe in the evenings. She lived alone with her cat and she took lovers and kept them as she wished. Her house was filled with music and beautiful paintings and pottery. She kept a guitar and a saxophone in her apartment for visitors. Her nights were too full of the thoughts and plans of the day to fret, and she slept soundly encircled by a constellation of brilliant dreams.

In the coffeehouse, one day, she looked up to see Diana standing there with a smile on her face. Diana, once again on the run to visit her beloved Europe, told her how fabulous Layla looked. "You're a real survivor," Diana told her.

"I've done more than just survive," said Layla. "I am doing well."

85

THE DISCORDANT PIANO

The first few flakes of snow fell with a series of premonitions upon the countryside surrounding Porkbelly Manor on the Ruching River. Edward was fastening his gloves at the door when Amelia approached to wish him off. Noticing his white tennis shoes and black gabardine she reminded him not to forget his rubbers, on account of previous errors, and kissed him upon the forehead. Edward, eager to be gone, and troubled by a vague unease, wished her to be well in his absence, and reminded her, in turn, of watering the fens. With a remark about their dear friend, Finnegan in Tibet, which touched upon a private joke of theirs, stepped out into the frosty air. He walked down the winding path to Poddington Road and began making his way towards the station at Collapsed Pudding, some two miles away, while high overhead a single star burned in bombast on and on.

In passing Deshabille cottage he could not help but overhear a conversation taking place on the other side of the hedges.

A man wearing a Worcester accent declaimed emphatically, "I say we should have the pond dragged immediately."

The other responded with a nasal Gallic voice that was wholly inappropriate, "Excellent conception, Msr. But if he is not drownded?"

"Ain't drowned?" interrupted a woman's voice. "If 'e ain't drowned 'ed of swum to the top by now!"

"True," said the first. "But what if he's drowned somewhere's else? He could have drowned in the Thames or Tibet for all we know."

Here, Edward gave a start as if jolted by an off-key performance of Cosi Fan Tutti. The Worcester man continued. "I say the first thing we do is drag the pond post haste. It's small and can be done in half an hour."

Meanwhile, Amelia, in making a jelly sandwich, was surprised from behind by Mortimer, the man-servant, who had changed costume from tails, tie and lined trousers to ski mask, leather jacket and cut-away chaps.

At the same time, in another part of the house, there was a murderous row going on between Patchouli, and Amanda. Perhaps unwisely, Lord Pushfront attempted to arbitrate the two. Patchouli disliked Amanda's virtual domination of the shower room and other house appliances. She thought Amanda should have some consideration. Amanda who lifted weights at the Women's Auxiliary in Collapsed Pudding, said Patchouli was a sissy, a limp-brained noodle, and a fool, and furthermore she should mind her own god-damned business. Patchouli swirled her beads and serape angrily before blurting that she thought Amanda possessed the manners of a South African howler. Veins stood out on Amanda's neck, and she replied so goddamn what. At least she wasn't a door lock for the likes of Jeremy -- Patchouli's current affair. In her opinion, Patchouli thought Amanda was piece of swiss cheese.

At this point, Lord Pushfront stepped forward. "Now see here ladies . . .". he began but got no further as Amanda shoved him backwards with such violence that he upset the nightstand holding the glass-encased brass fantod which crashed to the floor, shattering the bell-jar.

In the pause before the next retort they distinctly heard drifting up the stairs the hoarse-throated cries of someone who sounded very much like Amelia. After a moment, the moaning of a male voice intermingled with hers. Suddenly, there followed a rapid pounding at the door followed by a rattle of keys.

"Stop!" said Lord Pushfront. "I hear someone banging downstairs!"

The front hall door flew open to crash against the wall, knocking over the tall bottle-tree, and Edward rushed in past the flushed and breathless Amelia, who sat composing her mussed hair and skirts. Edward ran up the staircase without saying a word, leaving the front door wide open and astonishing the eyes of all as he continued up to the third floor.

Down below, Amelia was adjusting her blouse, when Mortimer appeared, fully dressed and carrying a salver of silver, which he set before Amelia, who hissed, "For god's sake button your trousers and look busy." Mortimer buttoned himself and then looked about. Seeing the upset bottle-tree he took it outside and set it on the flags after closing the door. He could hear a voice or voices muttering angrily from the round bay above. To appear busy and to hear better, he removed the hydrangea beneath the window and placed it next to the door lintel, where the plant nicely complimented the arcualia opposite. He hesitated a moment, but the voices remained indistinct, and so he decided to go get the polish so as to clean the brass studs beneath the window. He hurried around the corner to the back and down the rose-aisle to the im-plement-shed where the two gardeners were dis-cussing the fate of one of their fellows. "Yep, said one. "He was a dedicated chap who took what ye might say pride in his work. A real team player."

"Found him dead byunt," said the other. "Wit 'is trowel in one 'and, hydrangea in t'other."

"Tch, tch. He was a good friend of Finnegan."

"Excuse me," interrupted Mortimer. "Do you fellows have any polish?"

"Any polish? Do we got any polish? Damn! The man wants to know if we have any polish," the first asked the second.

"I'd say we do," answered the second. "Me mate's been to Harvard in the States and I've been to Eaton."

At the house, Amelia was leaning back on the settee contemplating the leftovers of a jelly sandwich that remained upon the silver salver when an un-earthly shriek like that of Edward Munch served an overdone flambe destroyed the relative calm of the house, and she turned to see through the bay window Edward plunge from the third story above to the yard below. Amelia jumped up to run to the bay window from where she could then see Edward impaled upon the bottle-tree, dead.

***

Much later, Inspector Gadabout paced back and forth before the assembled characters of Pork-belly Manor, humming "Les fossoyers sont joyeaux," while a team of experts photographed the scene, took fingerprints and dipped into the bowl of candied plums by the door. The inspector's assistants Finn and Watt, stood by, waiting for orders.

"This case reminds me of an anecdote about our dear Finnegan," said the Inspector.

Someone in the back row sniggered behind a handkerchief.

"Finnegan was at that time traveling in Tibet when he took it as a fine idea to ascend the tallest mountain in the world . . . "

"And he's still getting it up there," said a voice.

"I beg your pardon," said the inspector.

"You told that same story the time Lord Trotter was murdered in the abattoir," said Amanda. "And again when they found the curate in the brine vats."

"Astonishing you do not see the connections," said the inspector. "Finn, close that door. If you will allow me to continue . . . ?"

"Now see here Inspector. It's about time one tells us the meaning of all this," demanded Pushfront.

"I'm telling a story," retorted the inspector. "It doesn't have to mean anything. And it's better if it doesn't." Just then, there was a knock at the front door. Half a dozen cops leveled their revolvers and a swat-team equipped with pepper spray, tear gas and Raleigh bicycles prepared to rush forward under the cover of shields and batons. The gas was made ready.

With the stentorian voice of a basso profundo commanding the 9th symphony, the Inspector courageously took the initiative and bade Amelia open the door. Two men and a woman stood there in dripping clothes.

"Pardon moi," on of the men said. "May we borrow your dredging hook? We seem to have lost ours in the pond."

"Charles," Amelia addressed one of the gardeners." Would you please show these people to the implement shed?"

"Now then," began the Inspector. "Finnegan had taken upon himself the idea of ascending Everest, and for that he required assistance. Unfortunately, he did not speak the language well and instead of asking for 20 porteurs, he asked for 20 wallets."

There was an embarrassed silence while the Inspector preened his mustache happily with the knowledge that he had once again told the story according to his mind quite well.

"Did you ever catch the fellow who killed the curate?" asked Mortimer.

"What's a 'portmonnie?'" asked Patchouli. "I wasn't here the last time."

"Stupid git." spit Amanda.

Suddenly the Inspector stopped pacing and exclaimed that he knew who was the killer. Everyone in the room became attentive.

"Something unholy is loose in the countryside, my dear fellow citizens," he began, and promptly lost the attention he had just gained. "That something is here in this room with us tonight. Against such unspeakable horror, stands only the paper-thin line of defense, those doughty few who combat pernicious villainy with their cerebral gifts. I am speaking of course of the thin blue line. . . ."

"Oh get on!" said Amanda.

"Old cow." said Patchouli.

The Inspector coughed, continued. "Of all the people in this room, only one has no alibi for the time period in question for each of the murders.

"How could you know that," said Amelia. "You haven't talked to any one of us!"

The Inspector laughed like a triumphant Paglaccio. "I shall demonstrate through the amazing powers of inference how I have discovered the identity of the villain. And the identity of the killer in each and every murder case that's hit the books since 1865 and so doing, I shall overturn nearly every case which heretofore had been locked tight as a drum! Marple, Dupin, Holmes, the Hardy boys and even that fat little Belgian, have been entirely wrong!"

Gasps of disbelief.

"Finn! You had better close the door."

Just then, the lights went out.

***

Back at the station, much later, the Inspector poured himself a good dose of whiskey and put his feet up on the desk while Watt -- the Master Sergeant -- said admiringly, "How'd you ever scam it out, I'll never tell."

"Elementary, my dear Watt. There is only one individual who could simultaneously have committed the murders in so many places and still have the opportunity to cover his tracks so thoroughly.

"Patchouli comes from America and therefore knows nothing of us British. Mortimer is of the lower classes and is therefore incapable of action. Amelia is clearly mistress of the house, and has therefore a motive for murdering Edward, but not for killing the Curate. Pushfront is a Tory and Tories always hire someone else to do the dirty work. Of the two ladies, and I use that term, er, loosely, the both of them own decent, law-abiding bicycles. The gardeners, I saw by their ties, went to decent schools, which does not rule them out entirely, especially the Harvard gent, but the motive is lacking and such people invariably commit murder only when they stand to gain something by it."

"Marvelous! Bravo!" the sergeant said as he clapped his hands. "Still. It's a shame about old Finn. I understand he got clear away."

"Quite right. Once again the English countryside is threatened by the occurrence of bad literature and worse accents, although I suspect now that the heat is on, he'll head over to France or America, where they condone that sort of thing."

"When did you suspect him?"

"Ah, the power of inference, my dear Watt. I noticed a Labour party poster in his locker purely by chance, which gave me motive and suspect at once. Then in going to the scene of today's crime, feeling a bit of the pangs of the honest public servant who has missed a meal, I commandeered the man's lunch pail and discovered . . . this!" The inspector held up by its tail a small, complete fish about the size of a sardine, painted red.

"An herring!", exclaimed Watt.

"Perfect grammar, sir! Imagine: for years he had been committing murders and then coming in to assist the investigating officers after the fact when he could conveniently distort evidence at his leisure. He probably took fiendish glee in pinning the blame on some hapless Tory in the neighborhood by scattering enough red herrings so as to drive the poor rich bastards mad to the effect that many confessed to crimes they had never committed.

Just then a message came in that a body had been dragged from the pond at Deshabille cottage.

The Inspector looked at Watt. "Finn, again!", they said and rushed out.

The snow was still falling.

THE PAPERCLIP MAN

Mark lived a quiet life which he enjoyed. He enjoyed his garden, where he finally had gotten some decent beefsteak tomatoes to take hold, he enjoyed his apartment building where he said hello everyday on the stairs to Ray, and he enjoyed his beer on Fridays at the Golden Bear. For ten years he had been working for the Company in the same capacity, despite the pressures to get a move on, show some ambition, but all this changed the day his Supervisor called him into the Brown Study, the inner room of the Office and was told about Old Sonsini.

He had known Sonsini for a long time. It had been Sonsini who had been his mentor, and had brought him up, shown him how to get things done and set Mark walking on his own in the Company. Sonsini belonged to the old guard who had run things in the years right after the War.

They used to go out to the Stick to watch the Giants and there in the stands Sonsini, with a hot dog in one hand and a beer in the other, would give him pointers in a voice grated rough by years of old crow and cigarettes. He'd lean over and say stuff like, "Watch and learn. The game ain't in the runs, buy, not in the action. It's the pause between the strikes, the pause before the pitch." And then somebody would steal a base or slam a drive against the fence and Sonsini would jump up splashing beer and mustard screaming like a god damn maniac. Then he'd sit down and cram half a dog into his mouth and around the mash of dog and bun would come gems of pure paranoid wisdom. "You always got an audience watching, boy. No matter who you are. No matter where." And Sonsini would look up at the stands and the boxes behind them where all Mark could see was a slash of faces and glinting windows. "Son of a bitch. Let 'em know you know they're there. Don't fake it or you'll go crazy."

Now Sonsini had been retired.

Mark got into the car and drove over the bridge to the green hills. It was a clear fall day and the oaks had begun to turn color among the persistent yolla bolly and manzanita. Mark parked the car down the road and walked around the bend and up the drive to the house. A late butterfly wandered lost among the remnants of freesia and sage. Mark could believe, as Sonsini had told him, that deer sometimes wandered into the front yards to wreck the lettuce patches. "God damn communists with antlers," Sonsini called them.

Mark rang the bell next to the stanchion holding the American flag and Sonsini opened the door. He had gotten wider, stooped, balding, but he shook Mark's hand with the same old energy. The den Sonsini had set up looked comfortable with pictures of his kids, from girl scout age to motherhood set on the shelves with his favorite mystery and spy novels.

He came in and Sonsini offered him a seat.

He didn't want to slip into the way of thinking he had found himself in after the last job. Wondering about useless bits of detail, laying bets with himself as if the boredom of it was beginning to sink down whatever else could be felt. After the last one he had started wondering how many shots he'd have to fire; would it be one or two or would he have to squeeze off a third. This had stuck with him all through the job until it was over and then when it was over he found he had done two and then he forgot all about it until having to clean and check everything that night and somehow the memory of having occupied his mind that way made him nauseous. He didn't want to have to think about anything at all when he worked; he wanted his mind to be wiped entirely clean so that each new job would be really a new job, done automatically and done precisely.

Mark didn't say anything and remained standing.

"Oh. I see," said Sonsini.

They stood a moment until Sonsini started moving around the room picking up things and just setting them down, Mark watching without moving except when Sonsini picked up a paperweight from the desk; it was a solid gold paperclip encased in glass. Mark simply unbuttoned his coat and Sonsini set the paperweight down again.

"My daughter gave me that," said Sonsini.

He picked up a sheaf of papers pointed his eyes at them and then set the papers down again. The paperclip dispenser. A paperclip. A pen.

"I . . . whenever I was in the field, I would make these little men out of paperclips. Something to do while waiting maybe. You know how it is. One clip for the body and then a couple for each arm and the legs." He paused and Mark stood waiting. "I guess we better get going then, huh?" said Sonsini.

Mark stood to one side and Sonsini moved to the door where he reached for his jacket. They went out, Sonsini, without his coat, followed by Mark.

"My car or yours?" asked Sonsini.

"This way," said Mark.

They walked down the road in silence. Mark opened the passenger side of the car and Sonsini got in.

Mark started the car and drove to the freeway and headed south. Then Sonsini began to speak. Slowly, thoughtfully, the words rested comfortably in the car as they drove. First he asked a question of Mark. "Do you know Le Carre?"

Mark hesitated a moment before answering. "GM made that didn't they?"

Sonsini sighed, rubbed his face with one hand and said, "You are the whole problem with your generation." and didn't say anything more for a moment. "Le Carre was the only guy to get it right. Rumpled overcoats and bad livers. No chase scenes and too much goddamn standing around. Bad marriages . . . Remember Sullivan? Of course you remember Sullivan. Who could forget Sullivan. What a guy. Too bad he messed up . . . . I did all right. Twenty-four years. Two daughters. They're good girls. Vassar and Smith. Not bad, I would say. Both of them fine girls. Oh . . . they'll do all right. Scholarships you know. You have any kids? No. Oh well. It's worth a try. Of course we've had our troubles. Who wouldn't over twenty-four years? The secrets and ... well, you know. You know how they get, wanting to know everything. That stops after a while. Your wife now, you wonder what she is thinking sometimes. Do you wonder? When you are out in the field? Maybe your generation is different. Now the War is over. There is no enemy any more. No other side. Of course there's always an enemy. There's always another side. Always will be. As long as we have . . . Companies to run things. But its different now, do you see? The war is over now. It doesn't make sense now; we sit down with all our old enemies. All we did we did for your generation. We gave you a fresh start. Is there any generation in the history of man that can say that? We gave you everything. You have to admit that. We worked for you. We made you. We gave it all to you.

"You always gave away too much," Mark said.

Mark took the Old Bayshore exit and descended to the feeder road.

"Perhaps you're right. It came too easy. Promise me you'll read Le Carre. He tells it like it was."

The car turned onto Tunnel Road, which was potholed and cracked from the passage of dump trucks. The sun flickered behind the hills toward the ocean as he turned right and passed along a line of corrugated steel Quonset huts. He drove up a little unpaved road and stopped next to a chain link fence. They sat a moment without moving.

"I am proud of what I did. We helped make the world what it is. Your life . . . your wife and your kids, the ones you are going to have . . .".

"This is it." said Mark simply.

They got out of the car and walked a little ways into the field. Sonsini turned to face him. "I could run up right now into the hills, be on a plane to . . . to . . . Tahiti maybe and nobody would know." But when Mark still did not say anything he gestured with his arms out to the side, an old Italian gesture of futility, of recognition of despair. "We made you what you are. I am sorry Mark." He looked off to the side at nothing in particular. "Paperclips. They were just paperclip people . . . . I really am . . .".

In a little while, Mark got back into the car, alone, and alone he drove back along Tunnel Road to the Old Bayshore Freeway. The stars had splashed shotgun patterns across the sky, but Mark knew nothing about stars and he did not look or think about them. He did not want to think or feel anything at all.

Something rattled and clicked in the ashtray: the casings. He put them in his coat pocket. In the end, it took three shots. Something in him figured he would always be counting them from now on.

THE MASTER BAKERS

Once upon a time, in the land of the Midnight Islands, where the air lifted with the scent of good herbs and the people could still understand the speech of animals, there lived a chubby baker by the name of Faolain. Now Faolain stood four feet tall with thick, red whiskers and although no one knew his age, he seemed as old as the hills on some days and young as the dew on others. He lived in an croissant-shaped house built on the crown of a hill and each morning he rode a blue bicycle with a basket and dynamoelectric lamp to the bakery where he made glorious golden loaves, crusty baguettes, delicate muffins and other delicious things that everyone agreed were true works of art.

One day, while finishing up the day's work with his assistants in the bakery, each of whom was an officially designated Master Baker of Renown, anointed by the King and so forth, his especially industrious assistant, named Reuben, came up to him with a Grand Concept for a New Bread. Reuben, who stood a full two heads above Faolain and was as narrow as Faolain was wide, had a pencil mustache and numerous idiosyncrasies, such as the fact he polished his mustache each day with the same toothbrush he used for dental hygiene, and would frequently stop to think by standing on one foot with his hands clasped behind him. He owned what is called a "creative mind" and because of this affliction was always coming up with ideas, some of which seemed less well done than others. But since some of his ideas glowed with inspiration and took fire, such as the Grand Garlic-butter Loaf Concept, which turned out to have made a pretty penny, Faolain listened to him closely.

Since flour made the bread, reasoned Reuben, why not use flowers?

"Boss, I am telling ya, this could be big time!" Reuben said. "Just imagine! Hey! A Rose Roll! A Carnelian Croissant! A Lavender Levain!"

Faolain coughed. Said he would think about it. Which is what he said to every idea Reuben came up with. Then they busied themselves about the day's cleanup.

That evening, on Faolain's way home, he stopped beside a field and parked his bicycle against an oak and walked through the thigh-high grasses, collecting flowers -- some bright, some small, some large, some like bells and some like elves with wide open arms. He gathered bluebells, impatience, poppies, hyacinth beside a stream, honeysuckle, jasmine, freesias, sweetpea, woodrose, lupine, and, besides the myriad wildflowers of the field, he found a single, extraordinary, precious Rose of Jericho.

At home he spread this treasure on the table and nibbled upon a panettone, the great mind moving like a long legged fly upon the water. A pair of starlings watched from the windowsill as he set the Rose of Jericho in a dish of water.

The next morning he stopped at the field again on the way to work. When he showed up, he dumped arm loads of weed flowers, roses, vines and herbs in a multicolored pile upon the table. Reuben stood on one foot and tooted upon his mouth trumpet as the scent of meadows in spring wafted from the table.

A trial batch was to be made from flowers sorted from the mess, with a sample of each type of flower. Faolain set two of his trusty assistants to work sorting while he left them so as to take care of matters at the ovens.

Now his assistants, Siobhan and Michael, although industrious workers with hearts of gold each, had one particular character flaw of which Faolain was well aware, and which Faolain sought to rectify by having them work together.

Siobhan detested Michael and Michael reviled Siobhan. The fair-haired Michael wore a tunic of green and blue, which colors Siobhan loathed for some reason perhaps better explained by a 19th century Viennese medical doctor. In any case, the dark-haired Siobhan wore a tunic of red and orange just to spite him.

Wherever the one of them went, discord rose from the earth with spears and spiked helmets as if sown by demons as neither one could uphold a conversation without saying something vile about the other. When Siobhan got a parrot to keep as a pet, Michael bought himself a cat. When Michael won a footrace, Siobhan said he must have cut the course short.   When Siobhan lost a ring down the drain, Michael said it was a shame the whole hand hadn't gone with it. And so it went from day to day with bitterness and acrimony and lucky was the little person who escaped from the crossfire between these two.

Faolain remained determined that peace should reign in his bakery and so it was his intention that the two of them talk to one another, at the very least, and so he set them at the tedious task of sorting the flowers. Of course the two of them, for the exception of this one problem with each other, were the kindest, gentlest souls on earth. Siobhan would sit in the Feis-Mna glade playing the flute on her off days, and the little people would gather for gambols all about her and it was said that any person who heard the sound would fall in love at once with whomever they saw.

Michael, on the other hand, said she sounded like nails going across the blackboard and when she played, he stopped up his ears. In fact, he never went to Feis-Mna at all, remaining hard by Carriag-na-Fir by the sea, where his drum delighted the dolphin, the otter and the dryad, smoothing the waves for ships and swimmers of all kinds. When he did not play his drum, he painted pictures of hamadryads and city lamp-posts.

No sooner did the two of them get to work alone than the invective began. Siobhan complained about a bad smell ruining the flowers. Michael said it must be the reek of her armpits. Siobhan said it was too bad such a blind one as he deigned to paint pictures, being deaf and nasally obstructed as well. Michael mentioned he could hear her silly nattering well enough and that it remained an astonishment such a one so ugly had not been at least gifted with a brain.

With the sound of the big mixer going and the two of them sorting flowers side by side, Siobhan said it was fortunate the offspring of a jackass and a horse could at least work, but couldn't breed. Michael told her to go back to her mother, the hedgehog and her father, the goat. A wart on the face of the land, she said. He should go by night and ring a bell warning folk of his approach. Sheila na Gig, he said. Tinker's daughter. She hit him then with an handful of flour on his chest and said he had all the qualifications to spoil cheese and no wonder no decent woman would go with him. He yanked on a rose vine in her hand so that the thorns raked her skin and told her to mind not getting any of her on him with her diseases. She set down the vine and howled. Then she turned and grabbed his nose, calling him a stupid lout who should be restricted from the company of decent folk and school yards.

He grabbed her by the neck while she held onto his nose and the two of them struggled a moment like that until the table loaded with flowers went over with a crash. The flowers, sorted and unsorted slipped off and plunged all together into the mixing bowl with its great steel-bladed mixer still going around. The two of them separated and sct the table upright as the automatic machinery lifted the mixing bowl and carried it high overhead on the conveyor to the splitter. Siobhan called Michael every name that she could think of while Michael held his swollen nose between his palms. Reuben appeared at this point and the two of them accused one another of upsetting the table. Meanwhile the weed and flower dough passed in neatly cut loaves toward the rising area and the ovens. Reuben, incensed, sent both of them out to gather more flowers with peaceful Oisin and gentle Maebha, telling them that something had better change or it would be back to driving a delivery cart at four a.m. for both of them.

Up front, the counter had opened and the day's customers had come filing in. some of them had heard that something new would be coming out that day, Reuben being somewhat loose of tongue when he had a few pints in him and so they loitered, sampling biscotti and tea. Then, who should come in the door but the superbly tailored Conor Macroy who had come all the way from the City of Starry Bovine to sample one of Faolain's special loaves.

"I came a long way," said Macroy. "I want something Special. And I am willing to wait. A little bit."

Faolain, confident of great success, promised such a loaf as he had never tasted, smelling sweetly of roses and tasting better than dreams. Somewhat to hedge his bets, he also ordered several clever display samples to be brought forward. Not only was Faolain a Master Baker, but he was a savvy salesman as well.

While this went on, Oisin, Maebha, Siobhan and Michael entered through the back door with armloads of flowers. Something indeed had changed. A disagreement had developed over whether the trumpet flower was poisonous or tasty and now all four of them wrangled among themselves as to which individual would be the first to nibble and find out.

Reuben interposed and tried to stop the arguing without success. Several others in the bakery joined in, letting the automatic machinery continue its routine without monitoring. Up front, in the middle of a presentation of his Regal Chess-piece Cookie Set on Flat Bake, Faolain heard the sound of a fracas. He stepped away from the counter and opened the door wide to see half of his employees with Siobhan on one side of the bakery behind the oven conveyor, hurling day-old dinner rolls at the other half crouched behind tables firing back as fast as they could. One of the bakers on Micheal's side threw a batard shell filled with mushroom dip hitting Reuben in the head. The dip exploded mushrooms, cream dip and bread shrapnel everywhere. Someone seeing a figure at the door, grabbed a loaf just out of the oven and heaved the bread at Faolain's head, just as Macroy, behind the counter, said his patience had begun to wear thin.

Faolain ducked as the missile sailed over his head and struck the Judge of the City of Starry Bovines in the chest. Several of his guards lowered their lances at the loaf, which remained upon the counter where it had fallen.

"You have a unique delivery system," commented the Judge as Faolain closed the door. "If only my administrative assistants could work as efficiently." He picked up the loaf as Faolain looked on in horror. Instead of a beautiful, single rose color the loaf had come out all mottled with all the colors of the meadow flowers. "So THIS is what we have been waiting for. The loaf I have traveled many miles to sample. Rather unusual looking."

He gave the piece to his Official First Food Taster, who, if he lived, gave the go ahead to partake. The Taster nodded.

Faolain held his throat. The Judge was rumored to have sentenced one of his minstrels for a single bad note on an off rhyme to cleaning the floors of the Prison for the Deaf. Poor Faolain. His bakery was a shambles, his workers in revolt and his special project, ruined. The Judge obtained a silver penknife and cut off a slice of the loaf. He put a piece in his mouth. All watched with some interest.

The Judge grimaced. Faolain slumped against the wall. "Not to my taste," said the Judge. "Reminds me of sweet meadows in springtime when I was a boy. I hate childhood. No time for that nonsense now." Faolain sank down further against the wall.

"But the Duchess," mentioned his Taster. "Her anniversary comes next Tuesday. She likes meadows in spring."

"Ah yes, she does. Very well, I'll have a thousand loaves by Tuesday," said Macroy. "What do you call this thing?" he said to Faolain, who had stood up.

"Uh, Rainbow," Faolain answered.

"Rainbow? Grand. I like your style. Make it two thousand. Tuesday. Good day." And so Macroy left with his retinue.

Faolain rushed back into the bakery to find Siobhan and Michael going at one another in deadly earnest with dried baguettes that were to have been crushed into croutons. "Cut it out! NOW!"

The two of them, soiled with flour and avocado dip stood before the angry Master. "The two of you are henceforth busted to Delivery as of now! You are going to deliver a load to Judge Macroy on Tuesday to the City. Now clean this place up!"

The days till Tuesday passed quickly. Faolain modified the Rainbow recipe for a sweeter taste and kept the two disputants separated. Monday night, with the delivery truck packed and ready to go, he gave his delivery orders and sent Michael with Siobhan, together to the City of Starry Bovines. Several bakers gasped at what appeared to be an improvident action. Faolain however smiled, for he had prepared something in advance for the two of them.

On Wednesday, Siobhan and Michael returned, intact, with the truck and a pile of gold as payment. Holding hands.

Faolain had sent Reuben on Sunday to Macroy to inform the Judge of the entire situation. In the City Hall, Macroy had issued his decree. "Since no one else can do the job, you can keep each other out of trouble. I sentence you to be married together and god help your souls and your issue. And since you are musicians, you can play at your own wedding and this fete today. And you had better be good!"

With the judge sitting before them in the Great Hall of Judgment the two mortal enemies were given instruments and told to play. With the fear of the Judge upon them they each refused to look at one another for all the bitterness that lay between them. At the end of the long hall hung a great mirror and so they were brought to look at themselves at last. Siobhan's magic flute and Micheal's enchanted drum did the work and, of course, the two fell in love with one another, more or less, because in fairy-tales, the impossible always happens just when you expect it.

So the two combatants had been forced to harmonize at last and here the story ends. Almost everyone lived happily ever after, but then, real life stories seldom have happy endings anyway.

THE COLLEAGUES

Sydney, riding on high hopes and a dry martini lunch, came in whistling after cutting a sweet deal with UA. Frederick lounged in the leather chair, holding a scotch and soda in one hand and a silver forty-five caliber pistol in the other. Suzette perched on the armrest holding a cigarette.

"I found him," Frederick said. "I found Quentin."

"Nice." said Sydney. He asked about the gun.

"It's from the set," answered Suzette. "I am supposed to shoot a guy hiding behind some curtains. I am supposed to think he's an escaped con people have been talking about, but it turns out to be a mistake. It turns out he's really Managua's boyfriend."

"Serves him right for hiding behind curtains. Where's the Chivas? It's party-time." He found the bottle, poured himself a splash, then added more until the glass was full. Frederick asked if the deal had gone through and Sydney smiled, showing his teeth. "We are gonna be eating meat for a long time. Say, lemmee see that thing."

"I need that for tomorrow," Suzette said. "I'm supposed to get used to holding it."

"Bang poof!" Sydney said, pointing the weapon. "Poof! Poof . . . !"

The gun went off.

"You stupid ass," Frederick said. "It's got powder blanks in there."

Suzette held out her shaking hand and asked for the gun back.

"Oh yes!" said Sydney. "Oh yes, yes, yes, yes! WE are going to PARTY! C'mon, lets go."

With Suzette shouting after them about having to work tomorrow and who was going to pay for the broken window, the boys drove off in Sydney's new MG. As they came out of the hills, with the bottle on the seat between them, a police car with lights flashing raced past them going back the way they had just come and they laughed. "Our tax dollars in action." Sydney said. "Stupid fucks."

The car did a neat 360 in the street in front of a row of bungalows before Sydney drove up onto the lawn and while Sydney began hollering, "Pookie! Pookie!" at the house, Frederick mashed down the horn. A man wearing a blue vest came to the door and Sydney shouted, "Pookie! Get your camera! We're gonna go shoot a party!" Pookie came out carrying a minicam followed by his wife. Frederick kept pressing the horn, trying to play a burlesque tune with only moderate success.

"We found Quentin," Sydney said. "We are gonna go pay him a visit."

"Pookie," said the woman, as he got into the back seat with the camera, "Don't get into trouble again."

"We're just gonna ream an asshole." Pookie said. "Be right back."

"You and your friends. Last time they messed up mama's bedspread. How do you know he's an asshole?"

"Ma'am," said Sydney. "Will you cut with the god damn horn!" he said to Frederick. "He's a man who doesn't like his mother." With that, he reversed into the street and laid a patch going out, not hearing the woman finish saying, "What about my mother? Christ! Look at what you did to my lawn!"

Along the way, Sydney dinged a purple-painted lowrider while Pookie told them about an idea he had just sold to Arnold. Sydney whooped and said, "We are kings! We are fucking kings now!" A man wearing a gold chain and several tattoos got slowly out of the car, looking at them. Sydney waved the pistol. "Ride it back across the river, greaseball!", shouted Frederick. They sped off.

Frederick directed them into a neighborhood east of Los Angeles and said, "Roll 'em up. You boys look a little too pale to be seen around here." Pookie stared out the window and said, "I am sure glad you got a gun with you."

They stopped in front of a house in the middle of a row that had not seen landscapers or painters in forty years. A curving row of large pockmarks stitched across the front of one house, ending in a window boarded with c-grade plywood. In the drive, a '69 Plymouth sat up on blocks hedged by wild grass sown with dixie cups, broken glass and empty kleenex boxes. As they got out, Sydney edged an empty t-bird bottle into the street to join a pile of Cobra cans. A skinny woman wearing a red tank-tee and flip-flops and shouldering a little girl stood watching them.

"Aw," said Pookie. "Look at the little kid with braids and ribbons on."

"Make you happy in paradise, mister." the woman said. "For twenty dollars."

"Fuck off!" Frederick said. "Shoo!"

"Man, I can't buh-leeve this," Pookie said. "This is where he ended up?"

Sydney was looking around, a strange expression on his face, suddenly calm. Down the street someone handed something from a gray primer-patched Monte Carlo to a man standing in the street. Deal done, the car roared past them, squealed around the corner and was gone.

"It's something, ain't it?" Frederick said.

"I grew up in a neighborhood just like this," Sydney said. He took a hit of the Chivas from the bottle and passed it to Frederick. "Okay, let's go eat!"

They went up to the door and pounded.

"Quentin! Open up!"

There was an exchange of voices behind the door and a white man wearing a flannel button-down shirt and slacks opened the door. A Black woman wearing a white nurse's cap sat at a linoleum table. Baskets of sewing material and children's toys lay scattered on the floor, the couch and the bed.

"Quentin! How nice to find you at home!" Sydney pulled out the gun. "Now step back shithead!"

As the men filed in, the woman said, "We have no money!"

"We don't want your money." Frederick said.

"We're here to shoot a party," Sydney said. "We're artists. We make pictures."

"Frederick, follow her into the kitchen and get some glasses and some ice. And some water. You," he motioned to Quentin, "sit there."

The woman came back carrying a tray. Frederick came in and leaned against the door with his arms folded. He told her to sit on the couch and make herself comfortable.

"Pour Mr. Asshole a glass of Chivas. Nice and tall. We are here to party." He went up to Quentin and waved the gun muzzle under his nose. "You want water? You want some water, asshole? Don't just nod; answer me!"

"Yes."

"Say, 'yes please.' Say it! Use those fucking good manners of yours. Wait. Pookie, start filming. I want this all on tape. We can use the footage later. Okay now, say it. Say you want some water."

"I hope you have a good editor."

"I didn't tell you to say that. What kind of actor are you? I am directing you and I direct you to say, 'Please give me some water.' Imagine you are in the Gobi and you haven't had any for years. Now say it."

Quentin said his line.

"You suck. We gotta get you some method lessons. First, get him sweating a little. Fred, pour the man some water."

Quentin looked at Frederick calmly as he crossed over and poured water from a plastic juice pitcher into a glass. As an afterthought, Frederick placed an ice cube on Quentin's head and told him not to move.

"Man, he's cool, a real cool cat. Now don't drink any of that until I tell you."

"Looks like the onetime rebel has made it big time. You act just like an executive producer."

"I act like an executive producer because now I AM an executive producer, asshole! Or I'm gonna be soon. You have seen my movies. Admit it! You stood in line and paid eight dollars to see at least, -- at least! -- one of my movies. Isn't that right? You have seen my shit on TV., isn't that right?"

Quentin shook his head slowly.

"DON'T hand me that BULLSHIT! Even now you're still as full of yourself as you ever were. You and your asshole friends! Talking about me and talking about me and my friends while I lived in a cold water flat without heat for years! And you were off skiing and having parties and fucking your whores. FUCK you!"

"Is that your idea of success?"

"Don't talk to ME about success! Hey, I MADE it, dude. I can have anything and anybody I want. Everything I do is right and I have a car and women on the string while you jerk off in a fucking ghetto. Last night I was with Suzette until dawn, sucker. You know Suzette, star of 'Four Foxes?'" Tell him about Suzette, Frederick."

"She's nice," Frederick said.

"I bet you want to fuck her every time you see that show, don't you. Admit it; admit you want to fuck Suzette.

"I don't have a TV."

"What!? You elitist fucking pig! What kind of American doesn't own a TV.?"

"I can't afford a TV. or a VCR. I live in hotels where everything gets ripped off and I work shit jobs. Which, because of YOUR friends I get only occasionally."

Frederick laughed. "Don't lose that ice cube now."

"You can't work because you're fucked up. You're a fuck up and you always will be. We got jobs and houses and cars and women because, dude, we know how to get them and we are simply stronger."

"You're the establishment now."

"Establishment! You dinosaur! We give 'em what they want, asshole."

"Ask him about his mother," Pookie said from behind the camera.

"Does your mother own a TV.?" Sydney interrogated. "When was the last time you visited your mother? How come you never call your mother? Don't tell me your mother never goes to the movies. Look at you being taped! Doesn't that water dripping down look like sweat, Pookie? Cold sweat. Now admit it! What's your mother say about my pictures, pictures I KNOW she has paid to see!"

"I have never called my mother to talk about you or your movies."

Frederick leaned away from the door. "Will you listen to this asshole? Never calls his mother!"

"My mother doesn't like your movies," added Quentin. "There's nothing beautiful in them."

"Whaddya want: teddy bears, roses in spring and lovers kissing in the rain? Life ain't' like that pal. Hey, life isn't parties and intellectual crap. Most people don't give a flying fuck about Bergman or your French cinema. What is that? Intellectual bullshit for dandies and faggots. That's what you are: a pretentious faggot. Nobody has anything to say about MY life -- certainly not you." Sydney pushed the barrel of the gun up against Quentin's nose. "Listen dude. I grew up in neighborhoods just like the one you are living in now. Do you think that woman standing in front of your house gives a flat fucking damn about wild rivers and trees and trout fishing? I give them what they want and the proof is at the box office. Life and what it is!"

"I feel sorry for you if your life is filled with thugs going to meet Vinnie and Sal across the river, with failed bank heists, with guns, and with women who bleach their hair and act stupid to make a buck. You should see some of the people in my life," Quentin said heatedly.

"I saw one of them standing outside your door."

"That woman shows more beauty than anything I ever saw in one of your movies."

"I am glad! Glad! We got this on tape. This guy thinks a whore is beautiful! Man, she's gone with the clap and AIDS, missing teeth and she's got so many needle tracks in her arms, she has to push it between her toes! Are you fucking blind!" Sydney paced back and forth. "The only thing I find beautiful is my grandmother kneeling in St. Johns' praying for the soul of her husband. I make movies for people just like that woman outside and for your mother. The ones for TV. anyway. Now don't tell me your mother does not own a TV. set! And DON'T tell me a senior citizen doesn't go to the movies!"

"My mother doesn't go to the movies, Sydney."

"Horse shit!"

"She's deaf, Sydney. She's literally never seen or heard of one of your movies."

Frederick whistled through his teeth.

Pookie looked up from behind his camera. "I didn't know that! Did you know that? Holy shit!"

"I don't feel sorry for you. You still had all the best while we had to crawl to survive. Now I am so far ahead of you, you wouldn't smell it if I farted. You should be embarrassed."

"I'm embarrassed to be in this dialogue. It's as adolescent as the rest of your movies and your idea of success."

"Fuck you! Fuck your cocksucking pretentious attitude! You're the same as you were in high school! Get on your knees! God damn it, get on your fucking knees," Sydney screamed. He turned and snapped to the woman sitting on the couch, "You just watch!"

"This reminds me of a similar situation twenty years ago with Frank Fettuski. I guess you don't remember old Frank. This is good water," said Quentin.

"Put the glass down; do you think I am an idiot? I am counting to three. No, I am counting to two. I want you on your knees! Move the glass further away. That's right. Hands at your sides."

Quentin stood up slowly, tiredly. The two men faced one another a moment. A jet of water shot from Quentin's mouth and hit Sydney between the eyes. Frederick burst out laughing.

"I can't believe it. Man stands with a forty-five right there and he spits water at him!" Frederick said, doubling over.

The woman on the couch swung her arm forward suddenly and Frederick screamed. Sydney turned his dripping face to see the grips of a pair of sewing shears protruding neatly from Frederick's pants leg as if glued there by an Fx team. Quentin grabbed Sydney's arm and the two of the went to the floor yelling and kicking as the woman jumped away from the couch. The gun went off in Sydney's hand, singeing the upholstery while Frederick hopped on one foot after pulling out the scissors, falling against Pookie who had put down the camera to pull at Quentin, who was on top of Sydney.

"Just stop it!" the woman said. Everyone looked up to see her standing with a snub-nosed .38 revolver. "Get the gun," she told Quentin.

"It's just got blanks," Pookie said. Frederick moaned.

"I got two bullets, both of them real."

"Glad you reminded me about old Frank," Quentin said.

"Who the hell is Frank?" Pookie said.

"Frank Fettuski pulled the same stunt on me in high school. Caused all kinds of ruckus. You're not beginning to forget things, are you Sydney?"

"What are we going to do to them," said the woman. "I don't like being called a whore."

"Well, Sharon, they're in your house. I sure would like to show you characters some of the people in my life. But since Sharon has to get to work tonight, I can't take you around and show you the people at the Housing Authority, the guys down at the waste disposal plant, or the AIDS clinic, or the staff at the public hospital Emergency Room, or the workers down at the waterfront, all places I've had to work until your thugs chased me off and all people I consider to be every bit as beautiful as your grand-mother."

"I dunno about the E.R. staff. Now there's a possibility," Sharon said.

"Hey," said Frederick. "I need medical atten-tion!"

"Shut up. You want another hole put in you," Sharon said. "Well?"

"What DO we do with adolescents that go around with guns and cameras terrorizing the working world?" Quentin said.

"Hey now, it was all just for fun," Pookie said. "I gotta get home to my wife."

"Well, you can go. And you can walk," Quentin said. "Empty you pockets of your change, your keys and your wallet."

"Walk? Walk in L.A.!?"

"Take Wilshire. It's a long road. And you better take off that blue vest; this is Blood territory. Now git."

"Okay boys, let's go," Sharon said. "I've decided what to do with you. Honey, could you put some more of those bullets into my bag? Thanks sweetheart."

"Where you taking us," Frederick said.

"To work," Sharon said. "Which should be a novelty for you. I need someone to mop the floors."

"Sharon works for St. Emmas Inpatient Psychiatric Facility." He faced Sydney. "You will have experiences you can write about."

"Fuck your ass," Sydney said. "I'm walking out of this scene." He took out his car keys.

The doorbell rang. Sydney opened the door and a man wearing a gold chain and tattoos stood with several other men behind him. Several of them carried baseball bats. A dented lowrider, painted purple, sat across the street.

"Oh shit." Frederick said.

The man glanced casually at the gun in Sharon's hand. "You hit me," he said to Sydney. "I want satisfaction."

They stood a moment facing each other.

"Give him the keys, Sidney," Quentin said. "That's right. He's been a bad boy, he apologizes and he gives you his car. And . . . this car comes with a brand new minicam! There we go! Another satisfied customer. We have to go to the hospital now. Have a nice day. Bye now."

"You can bunk with Raven," Sharon said to Sydney. "He likes boys. Come on Gimpy. Time to go to work."

They exit.

BIG RED

A week had gone by with no sign of Big Red in town or at the bar. Jay had been coming in, acting strange drinking off by himself and not talking to anybody until it was giving everybody in the joint the willies. Friday night steamed in with banners and whistles and a hot little band featuring a gal wearing not much more than a wad of tricot over a pair of cowboy boots but still no sign of Big Red. Harley said he seen Alfred walking around town all week with a black armband on and then people got real quiet, talking in low whispers and this being O'Malley's, mind you, on a Friday night with that singer blasting the wall out with a whomping version of "Bring it All Home" and there Jay sat by himself at the bar like he had been doing all week.

Finally, Sharon went up to the bar, sat at the rail with her beer and quietly asked what the fuck was going on.

That's when Jay started talking, the low rumble in his voice from years doing the asphalt work down at Mason Tillman going like a Peterbilt while he told the story of Big Red.

"You know the way things been going down here with all of us and especially the way things were going with Red. We were down in the L.A. dispatch room, looking for a northbound job, when the Supe comes in with an order on hand and a smart little dude dressed in an Italian suit and pointed shoes.

'Boys, I got a live one here, a real ride to the glory hole. Here's two days work and 8 thou.'

"Naturally every hand goes up for that one, but the route bid, you know goes to the guy next in line. Which was a guy named Fredo, I think. So Fredo goes out with the Supe and the dude and they have a chat. Back comes Fredo, ten minutes later. Can't do it. Can't do a two day run for eight thousand dollars.

"Everybody else backs off, wondering what the hell is going on with this one, when the man won't do a run for eight K and him being a vet kept in a tiger cage for a year and a half during the war, except for Big Red, who flew choppers and downed two of 'em and who had just finished his last delivery up a dirt road at two a.m. in the hills where he had to back the sucker out, all 18 wheels for five solid miles. So he asks, naturally enough, what's the load.

'About 18 tons," says the Supe, with a grin on his face. He should have been grinning, getting that much weight from the railroad.

"So they go out and it turns out the load has to be split between two trucks and me being the next in line getting the smaller one, if you could call it that, of a double hitch. We drove on down right away to this new industrial park they got by the wharf and while the hitching got done the dude pulls up in a white Mercedes with another dude who was Saudi Arabian by the look of him, also wearing an Italian suit and these wrap-around shades that made him look like Arnold Schwarzenegger and when he hands me and Red manila envelopes containing the manifests I look down and see he's wearing a shoulder holster. Then he stands there by the car with his arms folded like he's waiting for Arnold and Rambo to come blasting around the warehouse while me and Red wash down a couple Macs each with that stuff they use for coffee down there.

"Eventually, they take us down to the container dock and everything had already been done up spiffy so it's time to roll. Man, when the clutch went down that bullet Peterbilt groaned, sighed and heaved with the valves going like a Halloween graveyard of singing skulls and rods pounded like the kettledrums of the Weehawken Symphonic. I looked over at Big Red's truck and saw in the afternoon sun an impossible quadruple hitch on oversize tires bolted to the back of Red's puller and the mother damn near spinning wheels on concrete trying to get moving. The Supe had driven down from the office, still with that big grin on his face ride down there beside the running board.

'What the hell is this?' I yelled down at him, and he holds out his copy of the manifest. I looked at it and then at him. 'Coi?'

'Coi. Yep,' he says.

"I looked down at my copy and there it stood, '10,000 coi.'

'Sam,' I says. 'What the fuck is coi?"

'Here's one right here in a bag as a test outrider. Almost forgot to give it to you guys.' He held up a plastic bag with what looked like a medium sized goldfish swimming in circles.

'It's a fish,' I say.

'Yep,' says Sam. 'Only the one's you got in there are a hella lot bigger. And more valuable. Some 20 thou a piece I reckon. All packed away in lead-lined boxes.'

'Fish. Twenty thou a piece for fish. That SOB back there is walking around with shades and packing heat for fish!'

'Yup. And he'll be following you the whole way, too. Him and his violin-playing buddies. And you best hope this little outrider gets there in one healthy piece or you're gonna be eating a hell lotta expensive sushi. Assuming your travel buddies leave all your teeth in. Here's the outrider. Here's the map. Have a nice trip.'

"Once we got underway, our Mercedes escort tagging behind, I got on the C.B. to Red and asked him what had spooked. Turns out Fredo's wife had run off with a sushi chef from Guatemala. The whole idea had offended the man's sense of taste. Which is just fine by me as the bills weren't coming in any slower and the extra cash meant a real evergreen this

Christmas for me and Wanda. And with those white lines flashing by I started to thinking about Wanda and a suddenly affordable thing from Vicky's Secret Catalog and how she'd look on the polar bear rug next to the fireplace and . . .".

"Hey!," said Harley. "This story about you or Big Red? Get on with it!"

"Jay squared back his shoulders and loosened the kink in his neck before taking a swallow of his beer. "I'm gettin' to it. Now some of you may be wondering about a few peculiarities in this whole business. The deviations from procedure being the least of 'em. And it bugged me a bit too, the least being the way everything got loaded on my own damn rig and no chance to check out the coupling at all. Just load and move out in a hurry. Well, I started thinking about some holy monk somewhere up on the other side of the Sierra sitting in the middle of a Idaho pagoda with slave girls and a fish-less moat and I just had to begin laughing. And I figured, well, mile 58 was coming up and with this load, no way we were gonna drive on past those scales. Time for checkout and a little self-assurance. So I start downshifting well before the scales and the C.B. wakes up with the guy in the Mercedes behind us.

'No stopping,' he says.

"Damn if I didn't have a shit in my pants right there. Red says no way he's gonna blast on past those Chips; they can just sit and eat their lunch in the car if they want and make it tuna, and the Mercedes just repeats the same message. So just before mile 58 comes the sign, 'Scales Closed,' so on through we go, no stopping. Then Red comes on the line and says he's got a problem. Don't we all. Red's problem, a problem you might sympathize with, lay in the simple fact that he was tired. He hadn't slept for three days, mind you, and he was so tired he had even stopped bein' horny."

"Yer shittin' me," said Sam.

"No kidding. He was running on pure alkaloid and nerve, speeding past the wall that's ever so close inside your head, burning the white line of energy down to the molten core . . .".

"Yer sayin' he was pushing the envelope," said Harley.

"Man he had pushed THROUGH the envelope and sent the letter to fucking China! And with those heaters tailing us there was not even the opportunity to pick up a hitcher, someone to talk and keep the mind awake. So Red says, 'Talk to me.' And I did. So we are just trucking along, passing Fresno, and me and Red are swapping yarns back and forth over the C.B. Man, we had just started and it was that song, 'The Post', going through both of us already. The sun is going down and we are headed north on I-5 and I am trying to come up with every joke and yarn and political-religious argumentation I could, because I wasn't doing too well myself. Can you dig it?"

By this point, the musicians had taken their break and had gathered around to listen to what was going on. One of them wanted to know who Big Red was.

"It don't matter and it do," Harley said. "He was six-four of the meanest and kindest soul you ever met. He had teeth made from a radiator grill, a load of slivers from a Vietnamese land mine in his chest and a steel pin in his knee from a little bike accident."

"Was that on his '54 Harley," asked Melinda.

"Naw, his kid's Huffey; a Volvo hit him while he was test riding it," Harley said. "And that was a '52 Indian anyways. He had so much metal in him, he set off the courthouse security system a block away. When he cut loose with his mouth harp, pieces of the ceiling tile shook loose. He came from hard time Stockton from his Irish dad who died of the asbestos and a mom who worked in the Oakland Housing Authority as a security guard. When he started his engines, the canyon walls of the city shook and inhaled to step back and give him room, 'cause he was the man who delivered whatever it was you wanted. He was the heart and soul of your deepest wishes come true, a messenger, a trucker, the all-night news and the mail man. He was the man who brings you that box you have been waiting for all your life and that's the truth."

"And a lover," said Sharon. "Don't forget that. When he made love . . .". She hesitated, looking for words to say, and then she just added, simply, "He was a poet."

They all sat silent for a moment staring down into the beer glasses. Then Melinda said, "Well, where is he?"

"Okay now," Sharon said. "Get on with it."

They all ordered another round of beers and everyone gathered around to here about the end of Big Red. Everyone in O'Malley's drew up chairs around Jay and the barkeep leaned over the counter to listen up. Even the musicians gathered up close.

"This was a long ride, as you may have figured. But white Mercedes and narrative conventions can go to hell when human nature makes its demands. Big Red may have been superhuman, but me, I got needs. I get on the C.B. and tell those dudes back there I gotta piss and I'll be god damned if I do it in the cab. And, to mention a little fact of life, after 400 miles, a man gets a little hungry. Which the dudes in the white Mercedes began to chunk a fit over, but there I was, pulling off on the last truck stop before Shasta."

"I don't wanna hear about your penis or your stomach," Sharon said. "I wanna here about Red."

"Well, me and Red are in the restroom of the truckstop and Red pulls out this thing that looks like a metal pen with an LCD on it. You know, one of those pen things with a little clock on it."

"God damn it, Jay" Sharon said.

"'You know what this is?' Red asks me. 'It was in the packet they gave me.' I looked at it a little closer and there, imprinted on the side of this thing was the word, 'Dosimeter.' I told him I had made deliveries out to Livermore and damn right I knew what it was. Then he told me to look in the packet and see what else was there. We came out, got some grub and our two chaperones hustled us back to the trucks to eat. In the cab, I opened up the envelope, and sure enough, a dosimeter lay in there clipped to a green Hazmat form and some papers written in Arabic. Now a Hazmat gets filed with the State when you haul something really nasty and a copy has to go with the operator who is SUPPOSED to take certain precautions. Well, most of you figured out at least by now that wasn't no fifteen tons of fish and water back there. It was fuel rods or something for the atomic testing site in Idaho: final destination. And there, there on the signature line, was a name with a lot of rank letters after it, stood the name 'O. North', and under the name, stood the title 'D.O.D. Intelligence Officer'. The dude in the Armani came and pounded on the door, telling us to get a move on, so I hustled them papers back in the envelope and we pulled out. It must have been close to ten o'clock and the driving lights of Big Red's rig burned in front, while the white Mercedes kept an even distance behind.

"Now I don't know about you, but when I do a job, I like to be informed ahead of time what the deal happens to be. It's not just social contract, my friends. It's just business. Now, as we head up the Alturas grade, Alturas being, mind you, a Nuke-Free Zone, I begin to put it together. North buys and sells drugs in Guatemala, ports the proceeds over to the far east, buys off the Iranians who are just about to blow the Iraqis, themselves and the Middle East to radioactive hell and then has to figure out what the hell to do with the stuff once he's got it. So, he sells your basic A-bomb to American industry to balance the ledger.

"All this time I am on the C.B. with Big Red, who says its a load of hooha whatever the story. Fact remains, we were hauling a hot load and somebody just felt a little confined by rules. My concern at this point, going over the Sierra ridge past Alturas, changed from the unsavory nature of the business to the issue that we had two hired yahoos dressed for the disco packing pistols behind us.

"We passed the brake check area, since there was no stopping, and ahead of us the road dipped. Big Red went down into the dip, going I guess about forty-five, then just leapt up the final crest. There was a loud bang at the crest, some smoke and piece of the rig went flying off to the side.

"It was a piece of the compressor unit.

"And so down he went. Big Red in his cherry red rig hauling near 20 tons or more, down from the top and down the steepest grade this side of the Divide with nothing to slow or stop him but the gears. I sped up, thinking I could get in front of him to slow him down, but a narrow sweeper came up and I had to let him edge away. For about a mile we did devil's tag with his running lights ahead of me swinging wide in the lanes as we accelerated down the gorge and the little Mercedes honking and flashing its lights as the dude chattered over the C.B. like Chip 'n Dale cartoon characters. I tried to catch him but the rig kept going faster with all of us running on too little sleep and too much coffee and bad food and the blatting of supervisors and the frustrations of all the bullshit until the big bend you knew was coming flew up and the rig, all 20 tons of it with Big Red inside punched through the rail like it was a bureaucrat's red tape and sailed out at over one hundred and ten miles per hour over the gorge into the dark. That's all I have to say on the subject. Little men with big guns have bade me to silence."

"He died," Melinda said. "He crashed and he died and that's all there is."

"This story sucks," Sharon said. "It makes me depressed and I don't believe any of it. Where's Big Red? Come on!"

"He's at the bottom of a smoking pile of radioactive wreckage," said Sam. "He's dead and gone. That's a fact." He made a noise through his teeth like a pig cleaning its lips.

"No," rumbled Harley. "That's not the way it was. You just do not understand. Let me tell you about how it really is. Big Red is not gone. I can see it now, those running lights of his in that darkness over the gorge and the moon shining down on the river below. Can't you see it? If you cannot see this, your soul has no eyes and you have lost your dreams. I want you to see Big Red's running lights blazing red, amber, white and blue above Alturas in those still pristine mountains of California where the water still runs clear from the Moses rock! I want you to understand that Big Red's truck, pulling the heaviest load that has ever been pulled blazed down and leapt from the road, not down, but up! Loaded with the most volatile fuel known to man, woman, child, beast or king, he flew up and exploded against the sky, scattering the incandescent stuff of himself against the milky way. When you go out tonight, I want you to see the sky as it really is: the running lights of a messenger who isn't any more dead than Joe Hill. God damn it, he was my buddy and a good man and the best there ever was!"

A little embarrassed, each of them separated, pulled their chairs back or left them were they were. The musicians went back to the stage and the bartender returned to serving drinks. All too soon, things returned to the way things always have been at O'Malleys. Except for a long time no one would go outside to look at the sky.

The bassist turned to the lead guitarist and asked what next.

"Straight ahead. Rock and roll," he answered. And they returned to work.

143

INCUBUS

He can remember the orange sparks of her eyes in the farmyard before she turned away. It was a cold morning. One of those cold mornings when the mist is still climbing up the cut of Carrickmines and the sound of the cow bells drifts out of the air magically so that you are uncertain, in looking towards the shrouded valley, that perhaps you are not hearing the predawn rhythms of Kingstown Harbor with its buoys and foghorns, but some other town with a different name.

She turned and stepped aboard the car as her sister got in the other side with the Irish setter sandwiched between them and her brother at the helm they drove down the little long gravel drive to the main road, where the green Escort paused as a school of bright-clad bicyclists shimmied in waves of blue and red around and up the road toward Enniskerry. Then, the car nosed into the stream of traffic and scooted away.

He stood in the yard, possessed by an incendiary spirit. He felt something happen in him as if every cell in his body burst with a fever. In a few minutes there would be nothing of him left. He did not know what it was, but something happened in that yard. The landlord's little red and blue sailboat in the corner became only a thing of wood and aluminum. The barn became a whitewash structure of odors and dark forms shifting against tether chains. Everything that had seemed so charming receded from his grasp, lost all significance for him. He floated, disembodied and disconnected. Himself, alone.

He fixed his view on a pile of roof-slates to still a wave of nausea. He climbed back to the cottage and lay on the floor with his knees to his chin in front of the fireplace. He wanted nothing, desired nothing, other than sleep.

From that moment, he felt old. He tried to do things that were young; he wanted to be childish and irresponsible and free of oppression. It was easy to be adolescent. He broke things. He annoyed people with long telephone calls about nothing. He spent long evenings spent sucking on a gin bottle. He refused to bathe for a week until even the cat stayed away from him. Then, he took a shower so that he could go into town and maybe kill someone in a bar.

It was no use. He felt tired. He slept most of the time. On the floor in front of the fire. A sleeping spirit had possessed him. He knew he was sick, but he had no energy to do anything about it.

Perhaps if they had separated in any other way. Perhaps if some kindness had been present then. Kindness which he had been able to recognize and remember. Or if he had not allowed her face, her eyes to burn into the landscape of his mind. In his dreams he could see the Escort glide up the road to the intersection, where a tractor popped into the back bumper, knocking the vessel into the path of a speeding double-hitched truck.

The car turned in his imagination successively into a chariot of fire, then, a tremendous St. Bernard, a refuse truck belonging to the city of Monahan, and finally a three-masted schooner tossing in the seas of a hurricane. The ship shifted about as a flock of seagulls arced before the bow, and struck a reef. As from a distance, although very close, the ship creaked, groaned (in howling wind, mind you) turned its massive bulk and canted over, spilling barrels, spars, rigging, whatnot over the splintered gunwales. Water rushed in and the prow slid into the emerald sea. The ship's dog hesitated on the deck before leaping into the splash and paddled in the chop before disappearing behind what remains of a grand piano. And she? Still in the lighted chamber, high up, as the ship's main cabin filled with water. The whole wreck turned in a slow revolve of fluttering red and white sails, screwing itself into the ocean until the high, lighted chamber eased down. Afterward, only a whirling screen of detritus, wrack and foam tossed this way and that, breaking up and sinking out of sight until nothing remained but the rain riveting the metal waves.

But something hauls that ship up out of the green grave. Because something does not want to imagine the scene in that chamber, something remains discretely aloof while afraid of letting go. The tossing of the fair queen roughly against the bulkhead, the shattering of glasses, the scattering of sacred objects beneath a deadly powder. And she is not the sort to remain passively enclosed in any case. She burst out onto the deck, stands clothed in St. Elmo's fire: saint, queen, angel. She becomes the incubus that will not die.

At first, it was like this: he runs down to the end of the little long gravel road -- ahead of the car -- lays himself across the way and refuses to get up. In this way, the fatal accident is avoided, she sees the depth of his emotions for her, she steps out of the car, they embrace and all is well once more.

Eventually, somehow, they iron out their differences.

Or, he runs back up to the barn, grabs a horse and rides it bareback, which he has never done before, over the pastures lined with stone walls to the star-bordered crossroads and stands in the path of traffic and so startling is the appearance that everyone stops. Same response. Same ending.

Or, he runs to the back lot, jumps into the landlord's Morris Minor, and races down the little long gravel road to the end where he takes a short cut known only to him to intercept the tractor in a terrific collision that geysers blood and metal and antifreeze and paper-bales for hundreds of yards in full view of the formerly fatal Escort. The three good-hearted souls run to the wreck. In surprise, she sees him, who she had just left, sitting in their ex-landlord's ex-Morris Minor.

"I never said I love ...", he begins.

"Yes you did," she says, softly. "Lots of times. What difference does it make?"

Or, in lashing rain, he sees the ship foundering on the reef from his lonely vantage point high on the rocks, strips off his waterproof, and dives from a great height into the waves to swim out to the wreck as a school of sharks shimmys in an arc in front of him. He nails together a quick raft made of pieces from the grand piano and pulls first her sister, then her, and finally the dog, singly to the shore by swimming with a rope held in his teeth. But unfortunately, she expires due to exposure.

In another scenario, he rushes to a hospital where her body, racked by terminal disease, rests in a sea of pillows. Billows of pillows. She looks so frail there, this ghost of herself.

Still, he returns to the ocean without knowing why. Perhaps it is the wind and rain we expect. The total experience of everything in an oceanic feeling. Or perhaps it is the sinking. The morning she left, the skies hung close and wet. The valley dripped. And her eyes collected every cliche in the book to throw it back at him with no defense. Everything, in fact, occurred almost wordlessly, as if each stepped through a program already rehearsed so well there could be no faltering.

In the end, everything that sank belonged to him and not to her. She crisply executed her exit with efficiency. The movers deftly wheeled the grand piano out like it was a five pound toy poodle. She had effectively removed herself except for memories and all that remained were a few photos, a few objects that without her loving spirit became gimcracks, plastic and porcelain detritus floating about the cottage until they disappeared or got burned or thrown out the window in a drunken rage.

It was that self-protectiveness that enraged him, because he realized that the more he banged at her door, the more locks appeared between them, until in the end, she stood removed behind family and friends and piano and he had no one, and nothing, not even self-respect. It was he, hanging onto a shattered barrel stave in the vortex. Everything just kept going around and around.

Of what use was a useless emotion at this point? he asked himself. He needed an exorcism. And so he ran out to Dundrum to get a bible and incense and candles. He lit the candles and the incense and burnt the lock of her hair he had kept. Oh, that had seemed so . . . flippant, somehow back then. Now he had matured. And so he returned to the wreck. As a seabird that flew into the window of the foundering ship, not to voyeur, but to finally exorcize the spirit.

She stood there, beside the table, which remained bolted to the deck as white papers, history books, building plans, slid off onto the floor. Somewhere a distant crashing: the Victrola. The bedclothes, green with wave patterns tumbled in a heap, became soaked. The captain stumbled by shouting, "Throw everything overboard! Lighten up!"

She ran to the bed and threw the bedlinens out the porthole. Then the coral earrings he had given her, followed by the green chemise. Then, her books, photo albums of the V & A Centennial, color-coded computer disks. The computer screen flashing an Union Jack burst in mid-air. Her furniture spun out into the darkness. Lambswool scarves. Grun's *Timetables of History.* Orange and green ribbons. UV bulbs popped among an entire alphabet of coalitions. The wicker settee on which they had discussed Virginia Woolf. The Cromwell diaries. India ink. Clay-potted plants hit the water like small bombs, the rose of Jericho exploding petals over the blue-green chop.

The captain ran by again. Waves were crashing over the fore-cabin. "It's going awfully well!" he shouted.

From somewhere midships, automobiles and motorcycles began pitching overboard with men lashed to the steering columns. A Ford Escort gleamed briefly before sinking out of sight. The piano hit with a tremendous burst of chords.

He could watch no more. She stood on the deck, her slim form drenched in rain, each line of her distinct. He could see the stretch marks of age, the knobbed hands, the crowsfeet, hair thinning as an autumn wheatfield. But it was no longer her smooth body that he loved, that he had wanted to possess. Or her style, regal and magnificent.

A burly sailor stumbled against her in running to the lifeboats.

"Asshole!" she screamed.

No, not a queen or saint any longer. But herself, and each forgoing death had been the discard of a packaged sentiment. The last was the hardest to give up, to toss into the waves. The woman who had called him "Bastard!", had crabby periods, and loved coffee in the morning, had few close friends, and who snapped at people at work. Whose grandmother had been at turns a tyrant and heroic. Who lied consistently and thoroughly about how she felt and what people said. Who liked to eat bangers and potatoes slaughtered in butter. Who shyly hid her head under the covers when making love sometimes. Who stood 5.25 inches in her socks. Who didn't at this point in the sinking give a fuck one way or another in her own pain about him.

"Asshole!" she said again as the seaman cast off in the only remaining lifeboat.

At that moment, the mainmast cracked in half and a loose spar from the foresail came down with its rigging to bang onto the deck and slide down the deck. Loose rope and tattered sail snagged him by the legs and he was dragged down, away from her towards the water while she still stood above, an electric poppy. Then the water closed over his head like a door.

A long time he rolled in a smoke of debris and water. In a dark place, he felt himself cough out the life left in him and he died fanned by leaves of whispering green five fathoms deep. His body convulsed as the spirit left him. While she remained above in light, he suffered a slow sea change.

On a fall day dappled with sea-borne clouds he swam up out of sleep, listening to the talk of birds. That morning an arc of swallows bellied out from the eaves and returned in cycles as he stepped out of the hotel and he walked in the open air among free men and women. He took the bus to the foothills and climbed the cindered path. Already, Sean and Macneice were at work on the site. The sound of spades and pounding and air compressors pulsed in the air. He would obtain another lover or another lover would obtain him; it did not matter.

He would build a new house to live in filled with things touched by others to give them life. The nightmares of the past no longer had power over him, because he knew the thing would always be there in him, following him as the shadow of the hand follows the harpist; it would never go away. So he breathed the air easily as he set about laying the cables for a home.

There would be a split in the power -- upstairs/downstairs. He had a nine-foot rod ready for the primary ground, and eight feet of cased copper. Oh-eight wire would run a secondary to the plumbing. Today, he was working on the inside; he had it all mapped out. The lead would go along the center support beam, along the roof-tree. He knew there would be troubles. Today he had to cut the cables with a saw because there might not be enough length to run from the DC transformer in the appliance room.

There would always be troubles; everyone the world over had them as a legacy. But he knew what to do about it and he set about his work, building the new house.

ORION'S BELT

So anyway, a number of years ago Bear rode his vintage '54 Panhead for a long ride out in the valley, talking the winding road that climbs up past the observatory and then down again to return to the Island out by Crab Cove, there to look across the water at distant Babylon's string of lights and the slowly easing sunset out past the Golden Gate, easing his mind from the rough handling that sometimes life metes out.

He was remembering a friend of his named Johnny, who had gone off to Vietnam in 1972 and not come back. And for a few others of his acquaintance. For Bear, everyday was Memorial Day, and the weird national holiday had nothing to do with anything in his experience. So there he sat cross-legged on a bench one Memorial Day, looking for all the world like some Eastern Guru. Until you got up close to him.

Bear remained the same as he always was: a swarthy man with one red tennis shoe on his left foot and one green one on his right, both diffidently fastened, equally mismatched socks of varying colors depending on what had been found in the drawer that morning or the previous. His sturdy legs sported denims that probably had seen the nineteen-sixties come and go by way of the manner stitches and patches held them together. Underneath something tattered, soiled, and disdainful which once had been a proud leather biker jacket, a tee-shirt that sometimes functioned dually as motoroil absorber and noserag adorned his ample chest above which a ferocious beard provided home for two full lips and an assortment of animal life culled from various alate species. He stored his Harley in the livingroom of his cottage next to the couch.

Some men, inhabiting life in such condition, would have found a lack of female companionship to be a bother, but Bear never had a problem with that issue. He was not without mates from time to time, but let us say those relationships tended towards impermanence. So it was a monastic life he had chosen and with that life he was content.

As the sun began to drop behind the striations of liquid incarnadine and gold shot with azure sky and white cloud a flash of green suffused the horizon. Just as old Orion began his thousand year hunt across the heavens a car pulled up and two people got out to amble over and gaze at the vista. All down the beach solitary individuals walked their dogs in the blue light, kicked sand in company, gazed seaward in a way only the mariner and the long-term prairie sodbuster understands, for out there is not field nor sea, but the eternal Big Sky, always worth looking at, especially when Life takes a sudden turn.

The man started up a conversation with Bear, which is no mean feat to accomplish, for you must know Bear was a man of few words, if only for the fact that Bear stored only a handful of those things within the etui of his mind. But this man was Irish, and, for all their faults, the Irish will never be at a lack of words -- it's their own response to . . . inevitabilities.

Look at the stars, said the woman. There's Orion, just like back home.

Which one is Orion, Bear asked.

The woman pointed him out and indicated the twinkling outline points. And that string there that's his belt. Or it could be his sword. Or something else.

OK, Bear said.

Was he, Bear, an American, meaning genuine article and all that pertains?

Yeah.

What kind of motorcycle is that?

Pause: mine.

And was that not indeed a genuine American motorcycle of the type storied and exalted in literature and film and song?

Yeah.

Well then.

You? English?

Heavens no! Irish. From Ireland. She by way of San Diego with short hops and marriage.

Married?

Married, yes. But not to each other.

O!

Well, let me explain, said the Irishman, whose name turned out to be David. The woman was named Danielle. David had grown up in abject penury, which in Ireland is quite a harsh thing for the weather is beastly and the people sometimes worse than the weather when they are your neighbors and aware of you. But a relative had earned a fortune writing children's books about a stuffed bear and his friends and this relative had developed a great wish for David, who got sent off to school where they discovered the boy actually had talent! In music of all things! One thing led to another (this story would itself comprise a short novella) and David became quite the star in the firmament of Irish classical music, working his way, if it may be called that, to full orchestral conductor. With success comes the dutiful marriage and the wildly undutiful spouse, soon dispensed with in typical Irish fashion, with a house and income and orders never to show her face.

This was, of course, when the Republic was predominantly Catholic, and not the hotbed of liberal sin and divorce it has become.

Danielle had longed to escape the drab sandy hot dry confines of San Diego and so had cultivated her own musical abilities, soon gravitating to Ireland, as becoming a member of the Staatskappele in Wien, Berlin, Bonn, Paris, London, Tokyo, Beijing or any of the great cities involved standing in line a long time and worshiping, in turn, someone's personal Priapus.

So she was a flautist and gorgeous and people noticed. The world of performance is difficult and you do what you have to do. So she took up the harp.

Easier to say, "Sorry Sir, I simply cannot do what you wish."

O the scandals of the classical music world she could unveil! The atrocious bestial habits! The carnality! The fiddling!

So she found herself in dear dirty Dublin, the Ford of the Hurdles. To stay in country as a musician she conveniently married an Irishman who turned out to be conveniently driven with the hots for Eton male graduates. They never lived together and so that was that -- she got her residence card, and because divorce was illegal, she remained Irish until death. Her husband possessed all the cover he needed to chase after apple-cheeked boys in short pants. But what was a girl in the prime of life to do with all her boundless energy?

She did what all reasonable Irish did in those days: she met David who was handsome, charming, affectionate and moved in with him to make what the Church and State still could not figure out -- harmony instead of Matrimony. They had bearskin fur comforters on their bed made in Bulgaria to keep them warm. For a while fur kept them warm.

Well that story lasted only so long. There is some kind of income for the Kappelemeister of Dublin, but coming from the sort of background he had, David also wanted to do some good in the world and so David took on as a part time sort of thing this choirmaster for a boy's school in Belfield. These two occupations occupied most of his time and of course, there were in the late nights opportunities offered to the handsome Kappelmeister.

As for Danielle, she was quite a hot pistol coming to dear dowdy Dubh Linn after traveling all over the world. O she did the charity work for the Magdelenes in their laundries and she took on the troubles of the wives living close by and sheltered them during the times of red devils in the bed and all hell breaking loose and all regarded her as the saint and soul of all things good.

They lived together in a large house set up above some peaty woods with a gameskeeper's cottage down below they sometimes put out to let for students. And for a while, everything was just tops.

Well you know how it goes. Nothing continues forever, not even goodness, for even goodness can go stale, get boring. The brief infidelities. The shouting and the recriminations. The loud arguments of which the Irish are surely the champions. Then comes the dreadful moment when there is the handslap to the face. The overt threat. Shouting and worse. Screaming and shattering of things. The common recognition that Life does not go according to plan. Public insults. Door slams. Anger swells in the close rooms fueled by peat fires in the once homey hearth and requirements. How could you. You ass. Her voice, once the delight of sopranos turning into a shrill harpy's shriek. Smashing crockery. The mild-mannered Choirmaster of a boy's school found himself raising his angry fist to strike. The bestial . . .

Danielle found herself traveling down the hall with a large cleaver in her hand to enter the amber-lit room to find David sobbing beside the harpsichord with his head in his hands.

The pistol lay on the bed beside him. His hands looked tired and old as they held his bearded head, heavy, so heavy. How had things come to this?

Now was the time for a vacation. Perhaps their last together. Trying to figure things out. Looking for a sign.

So there they were at the ends of the world, their common law marriage falling apart and Orion wheeling overhead from where the arrowshot had put him with his mysterious belt. Everything was finished, everything ruined.

And there sat Bear, listening. I know hard people.

Yes. Of course, David said.

You aren't like that. I see two good people. You describe two strangers. Ask your friends -- is this you? No. Everybody knows. How did you get here?

Uh, said Danielle. We flew.

Nonstop?

Uh I think we changed planes in . . . Chicago. Was it Chicago or Kansas?

I think it was Chicago, Danielle said. It was an airport.

So you come all this way sitting together and here you are. You don't want to break this up do you?

Silence.

Go home. Meet again. Move. Start over. Talk about those bad people you knew that did bad things. Those other people.

Well, David said. Well.

That wasn't him, was it, Bear said to Danielle. You know him. That was someone else.

Righ', Danielle said.

Look out there for a while, Bear said, meaning the darkening bay with the constellations marching overhead. You came a long way. And he got up and started up his motorcycle and before leaving them there he said, Go home. Become something other than what you became.

Then he left the couple there and they were silent a long time. Eventually they got back in their rental car and drove away and continued their trip up the California coast, not saying much to each other, thinking. When they got back to their place on the outskirts of Dublin they moved out of the big house and put it up for rent. David moved into an apartment in town. Danielle moved into a cottage on the edge of a village named Kilternan.

They changed their names to names which are not recorded here. The man who had been David showed up on the cottage doorstep ringing the bell.

The woman who had been Danielle opened the door and exclaimed, "What on earth! Did you lose your keys?"

"Hello," the man who had been named David said. "My name is ----------. Would you like to come live with me?" And he gave her a spray of gorgeous flowers.

"Well . . . I don't know you very well. Perhaps we should go on a date and get to know each other first," the woman said.

And so it began. The two people went out to a restaurant, and the next night to a movie, and then to a play. And after a few restaurants and seeing a few plays and which featured a sleep-over in the latter days, their relationship blossomed.

The woman who had been Danielle quit her job, snipped a few loose ends, employed different tradesmen, and became the other person that was herself, her real self. A person passing on the street might call out a name, but she kept on, and if they persisted, it was "I am sorry, do I know you from somewhere?"

And so that is how the story went. Friends were very puzzled and of course for a while telephones and such things were a tremendous problem. You see those people, well they were awful and we do not deal with them anymore, or as little as possible. The school took things in stride. The man who had been David told them that a dear relative who had written children's books about the adventures of a stuffed bear had passed away and he had taken on the man's name for sentimental reasons. Well with reasons like that, you can go far in Ireland to be sure.

After a courtship that lasted nearly a year, Danielle moved in with David to a little cottage that had once been a gamekeeper's lodge on the grounds of a big house owned by a couple who were reputed to be very bad to one another, but who nobody ever seemed to see out and about. The cottage was small, snug, and the piano filled what passed for the diningroom/livingroom. The big house had been put out to let by artists and musicians.

It's not easy assuming a new life; you don't just don't don one like an overcoat, but in this case it was worth it. Everyone who met them commented what a lovely couple they were. As for that other couple that used to live in the big house up the hill, well. . . . We don't talk about them. We just know they are still there.

ABOUT THE AUTHOR

Denby Montana has trundled about the American West, performing odd jobs here and there and acquiring academic degrees much as an hamster collects nuts. He has been variously a cowboy, a rustler, a bar keep, a repo man, an athlete, an actor, a roustabout, a graphic artist for T-shirts, a musician, a computer repairman, a mountain climber, a bicycle messenger in San Francisco, and a ne'er do well. He currently resides on an island set in the San Francisco Bay which also home to a gaggle of malcontents, dissidents, ex-Hells Angels and gypsies.